To desire a thief...

Daniel reached Aldridge's office and went inside. What greeted him made him stop in his tracks. "Miss Renwick?"

She stopped, her hand on the desk drawer she'd just closed. Dots of pink colored her cheeks. She would have looked alluring if she hadn't also looked guilty. "Good evening, my lord. I do believe I'm in the wrong room."

The constable in him roared to the surface and he closed the door. "What are you looking for in Lord Aldridge's office?"

"Nothing. As I said, I'm in the wrong place. I was looking for the retiring room." She moved around the desk.

Daniel stepped into her path. "You thought the retiring room might be contained in the desk drawer?"

The pink in her cheeks darkened and spread. "Of course not. If you'll excuse me." She made to move past him, but he placed his hand on her forearm.

"I will not. At least not until you tell me what you were doing. You were looking for something. Tell me what it was."

She moved away from him as if his touch burned her. Maybe it did. The feel of her skin beneath his palm was enough to heat him in the most inappropriate places.

"Please, I was mistaken." Then she dashed for the exit.

Daniel went after her, but she'd already opened the door and was stepping into the corridor. He stopped short lest he tackle her over the threshold, but then she spun on her heel and charged right back into him, sending him stumbling backward. She gained her balance, turned, and shut the door firmly.

Daniel lurched forward and, without thinking, pinned her against the door. He laid his palms on either side of her shoulders against the wood. "What the devil is going on?"

"Keep your voice down," she hissed. "Someone is in the corridor."

He didn't move away from her. Instead, he enjoyed the heat of her body, the flush of her exertion, the shallow pant of her breath. She kept her eyes averted, but Daniel would get her to look at him soon enough.

"Unless you want me to open this door and let all and sundry see us together, you'll tell me what the hell you were doing in Lord Aldridge's office."

Also by Darcy Burke

Her Wicked Ways

His Wicked Heart

To Love a Thief (a novella)

Never Love a Scoundrel

Scoundrel Ever After (September 2013)

Praise for Darcy Burke

Her Wicked Ways

"A bad girl heroine steals both the show and a highwayman's heart in Darcy Burke's deliciously wicked debut."
—Courtney Milan, *New York Times* Bestselling Author

"Captivating and romantic. Miranda is my favorite kind of heroine—witty, resourceful, and a little bit wicked—and I loved Fox for loving her as I much as I did."
—Jackie Barbosa, Award-Winning Author

"…a delightful romance mixed with humor, tenderness and love."
—Rogues Under the Covers

"…fast paced, very sexy, with engaging characters."
—Smexybooks

"Sexy and wonderfully romantic. Her Wicked Ways is a debut every fan of historical romance should add to their to-be-read pile!"
—The Season

"FANTASTIC characters…totally recommend this delightful Regency romance…"
—Romancing the Book

"What a wonderful debut! Highly entertaining…the pages sizzle with sexual tension."
—Forever Book Lover

His Wicked Heart

"Intense and intriguing. Cinderella meets *Fight Club* in a historical romance packed with passion, action and secrets."
—Anna Campbell, *Seven Nights in a Rogue's Bed*

"A romance that is going to make you smile and sigh…a wonderful read!"
—Rogues Under the Covers

"The storyline was fresh with a cast of well developed characters. Darcy Burke is an author on the move!!"
—Forever Book Lover

"I loved the book: interesting storyline, wonderful characters, and a touch of humor. 5 stars."
—Booked Up

"You'll love this incredible story of trial and triumph!"
-Kerrific Online

To Seduce a Scoundrel

"Darcy Burke pulls no punches with this sexy, romantic page-turner. Sevrin and Philippa's story grabs you from the first scene and doesn't let go. To Seduce a Scoundrel is simply delicious!"
—Tessa Dare, *New York Times* Bestselling Author

"An enthralling tale of adventure, passion and redemption. At times humorous and at times deeply touching, To Seduce A Scoundrel is a unique tale with a sexy hero you will never forget."
—Leigh LaValle, *The Runaway Countess*

"A great read with a gorgeous tortured hero and a surprisingly plucky heroine, I can't wait to read Ms. Burke's next book."
—Under the Covers Book Blog

"A delicious blend of love and acceptance, humor and angst, action and heat, and a book I would recommend for any historical romance fan!"
—Rogues Under the Covers

"I was captivated on the first page and didn't let go until this glorious book was finished!"
—Romancing the Book

To Love a Thief

"With refreshing circumstances surrounding both the hero and the heroine, a nice little mystery, and a touch of heat, this novella was a perfect way to pass the day."
—The Romanceaholic

"This novella has it all--action, romance, love and passion…a lovely story!"
—Rogues Under the Covers

DARCY BURKE

To Love a Thief

Copyright © 2012 Darcy Burke
All rights reserved.
ISBN: 1939713013
ISBN-13: 978-1939713018

This is a work of fiction. Names, characters, places, and incidents are the product of the author's imagination or are used fictitiously. Any resemblance to actual events, locales, or persons, living or dead, is purely coincidental.

Book design © Darcy Burke.
Cover design © Patricia Schmitt (Pickyme).

All rights reserved. Except as permitted under the U.S. Copyright Act of 1976, no part of this publication may be reproduced, distributed, or transmitted in any form or by any means, or stored in a database or retrieval system, without the prior written permission of the author.

For Emma, my first CP and one of the very best friends a girl could have.
I'm so glad we found each other.

Acknowledgements

I was a little daunted by writing a novella, but darn if it wasn't tons of fun. Thank you to Emma, Rachel, Elisabeth, and Erica for reading and making it the best little book I've ever written. (Yeah, it's also the *only* little book I've ever written.) And thank you Morgan Sneed for beta reading with a wonderful eye (and lightning fast too!).

Thank you Martha Trachtenberg for your fabulous, fabulous copyediting—you are a gem! Another thank you—and a massive one at that—to Lucinda Campbell who is quite simply amazing. Also, special thanks to Steve for reading. Or at least trying to. One of these days you'll get it.

And thank you to my wonderful children, whose patience and love continue to amaze, inspire, and humble. I love you.

Chapter One

May, 1818, London

JOCELYN RENWICK had loved a good ball—the dancing, the decorations, the costumes, the breathless excitement as guests arrived—during her very brief Season two years before. She'd been full of wonder and anticipation for a future that had seemed rife with possibility. Now, as a paid companion, she adorned the wall, and the balls she'd once enjoyed had become sadly lackluster.

It wasn't that the balls themselves had suddenly turned dull. It was her situation. With no close relatives to turn to after her father's death, she'd become the ward of a family friend, who'd inherited Papa's property and meager estate. While her guardian had taken care of her, he hadn't offered to finance another Season, and her trust wasn't sufficient to cover the expense. And since there was no one marriageable—at least in her opinion—in her small village in Kent, Jocelyn's options were limited.

She'd jumped at the chance to serve as paid companion to her guardian's great-aunt, Gertrude Harwood. She was a charming, elderly widow, and Jocelyn was delighted to accompany her for what she said might be her final Season.

Unfortunately, Jocelyn's Season so far hadn't included meeting any eligible bachelors or any dancing. The only people she mingled with were Gertrude's friends, who were even now clustered about.

The edge of Mrs. Montgrove's monstrous fan—it was the size of a dinner plate with ostrich feathers jutting at all angles—caught the side of Jocelyn's head, dislodging a lock of hair.

"Oh!" Mrs. Montgrove turned to Jocelyn with eyes widened in horror. "I'm so clumsy. Look what I've done to your coiffure. Here, let me fix it." She tried to smooth the hair back up toward the rest of the curls styled atop Jocelyn's head. However, judging from the tickle against her ear, the wisp wouldn't stay put.

Mrs. Montgrove's brow furrowed.

"Just tuck it behind her ear," Gertrude said with a wave of her fan, which was decorated with small diamond-shaped mirrors.

"Let me." Mrs. Dutton removed her glove and then licked her finger. When her digit moved toward the wayward lock, Jocelyn had to fight to keep from ducking.

Instead, she held up her hand. "I think I'll just repair to the retiring room for a spell before the rest of my hair falls apart."

They all stared at her, and Mrs. Montgrove looked stricken.

Jocelyn rushed to add, "It's not your fault. My hair has a mind of its own." She gave all of them her sunniest smile before turning on her heel and picking her way through the ballroom. She hadn't meant to imply that Mrs. Montgrove had caused a hair disaster. Someday she would perhaps learn to think before she spoke; however, the task seemed especially difficult when neither Mama nor Papa were around to offer loving reprovals.

Oh, how she missed her parents. Tears blurred her eyes as she meandered through the crowd. Mama had been gone a very long time, but Papa's death just two years ago was still fresh enough to elicit a sharp twinge of melancholy, if only for a moment.

She shook the emotion off. Her eyes refocused, and she attempted small smiles as she passed people she'd met two years before. Some made eye contact, while others simply looked away or stared right through her. There was nothing like an aborted Season followed by two years of mourning and adjusting to a life without family to make one feel insignificant.

Oh, Papa. Jocelyn made it out of the ballroom before her throat dried up and constricted. Perhaps she'd returned to London too soon. Perhaps she shouldn't have come back at all.

By the time she reached the retiring room she'd mostly recovered her equilibrium, locking her grief in the recesses of her mind. Pasting a pleasant expression on her face, she opened the door and immediately stepped to the side as a woman departed. She skirted by Jocelyn without making eye contact.

Invisible. No one saw her and they never would, for she hovered at the fringe of polite Society as a paid companion. Still, it was better than nothing, and without the funds to finance a second Season, the best she could hope for. She was young, and perhaps she'd yet marry.

Straightening her spine and again banishing her maudlin thoughts, Jocelyn closed the door and moved into the retiring room. An attractive brunette was patting her hair before a mirror. She turned upon hearing Jocelyn's approach and offered a friendly smile. "Good evening."

Jocelyn was momentarily surprised. Her lips curved up in response and then froze as her gaze settled on the necklace around the woman's neck. Three strands of pearls were held together by an oval, ivory pendant, which bore a hand-painted scene of two lovers in a boat beneath a sweeping willow tree. Her *mother's* necklace—it had to be—the one Papa had commissioned as an engagement gift. Jocelyn squinted, looking for the scratch in the glass over the ivory—damage caused by her tiny fingers when, as a toddler, she'd knocked it off Mama's dressing table.

Seeing the small defect, Jocelyn was instantly transported back two years to the night she and Papa had returned home after a musicale to find their house ransacked, their retainers bound together in the scullery, and all of their most prized possessions gone. The panic and fear came back to her in a wave, as did the shock of her father's heart attack that had occurred as a result.

But that was then. Now she was safe and whole, even if Papa wasn't.

Somehow, Jocelyn found the ability to speak calmly though her heart was racing. "What a lovely necklace. Wherever did you find such a treasure?"

The woman's fingers came up to touch the pendant, and Jocelyn had to suppress the urge to snatch the piece from her neck. "My dear husband gave it to me. It's quite special, isn't it?"

Before Jocelyn could make further inquiries, the woman swept past her and exited the retiring room. Jocelyn whipped around and made for the door. It opened inward, causing Jocelyn to jump back to avoid being caught by the edge of the wood.

Two women, deep in tittering conversation, bustled in, forcing Jocelyn to step to the side before she was trampled. Invisible again.

As soon as the way was clear, she rushed into the corridor, but didn't see the woman wearing her mother's stolen necklace. She hurried back to the ballroom, desperate to find her. Once inside, she stopped short. Blast! There were so many people. And too many blue gowns. Jocelyn's quarry wore a cerulean gown with ivory flounces at the hem.

Keeping her gaze moving over the crowd, Jocelyn made her way in the direction of Gertrude and her friends. With her attention so focused on her hunt, she failed to notice the foot she trod upon until it was too late to avoid.

"Pardon," said a deep, male voice.

Jocelyn nearly stumbled, but a strong hand clasped her elbow and kept her from sprawling face-first in the middle of the ballroom. She regained her balance and turned toward the man she'd offended.

An exceptionally white cravat met her gaze. She looked up and up—he was quite a bit taller than she, an easy feat given her diminutive stature—and stopped when she met his dark blue-gray eyes. She'd expected to see annoyance and was surprised, for the second time that evening, when they crinkled in amusement.

"You look as if you're on a mission. May I be of service?" He offered his arm.

Jocelyn stared at his sleeve as she tried to pull her thoughts from finding the woman in her mother's pendant and refocus them on the first gentleman she'd met in two years.

He leaned down slightly and whispered, "Please take it lest someone think I'm waiting for a bird to land."

Unused to a gentleman's attention, let alone one with a sense of humor, she arched a brow at him. Then she quickly wrapped her hand along his forearm. "We wouldn't want that," she murmured.

"Now, where may I escort you?" In addition to being tall, he was quite handsome, with broad cheekbones and a wide chin with a small cleft in the center. "Or, shall I be lucky enough to secure a dance?"

A dance? The first dance she'd been offered in two years and she said, "No, thank you, I need to find someone." The flicker of disappointment in his gaze made her rush to add, "I should be delighted to dance with you after I find…" Her brain stalled a moment as she tried to think of something to say other than "the woman who stole my mother's necklace." "My friend, Mrs. Harwood. I am just returned from the retiring room and want to ensure she doesn't worry after my absence."

He inclined his head, which was covered in thick dark hair cut a trifle shorter than was fashionable. It suited him. "Just tell me where to go so we may reassure your Mrs. Harwood, and then we'll have our dance."

Drat. Or maybe not. She could use the opportunity of their dance to locate the woman in the blue gown without wandering the room alone. And, oh, to dance again! "Just over there, near the corner," she said.

He guided her through the throng. "I realize we haven't been properly introduced, but I'll accept your assault on my toes as an adequate reason to dodge propriety, if you don't object?"

The whole was said with such wit that she smiled in spite of her anxiety over seeing her mother's pendant. "I can't possibly object to that. Thank you for your generous consideration, sir."

"Lord Carlyle at your service," he intoned deeply with a nod of his head that was surely meant to take the place of a bow, which he couldn't possibly execute during their cross-ballroom circuit.

Lord Carlyle … Jocelyn searched her memory for the name from her Season. She hadn't heard of him at all, which wasn't surprising. She'd attended only a half-dozen social events before her world had turned upside down.

"I'm Miss Renwick," she said, dipping her knees as they walked, in a sort of awkward, mobile curtsey. Perhaps she should have just inclined her head, too.

"A pleasure to make your acquaintance." His voice was deep and a bit raw. That is, his tone was not the same as other gentlemen she'd met in Society. She couldn't quite put her finger on it, but Lord Carlyle was somehow different. He even looked different. Oh, his cravat was perfectly tied, but there were no jewels sparkling from the folds, no ring adorning either hand, and no watch fob to spark conversation. An image of the fob Mama had given Papa as a wedding gift flashed in her mind. It, too, had been stolen.

Remembering her mission, as Lord Carlyle had called it, she glanced about for the woman in the blue dress. Where had she gone?

They broke free of the crowd as they came to the less-populated corner of the cavernous ballroom. A handful of potted trees were clustered like a makeshift forest, in which Gertrude and her friends were gathered.

Gertrude's head bobbed up and down. Her body sometimes succumbed to fits of shakiness due to her age. "Ah, there you are, dear. And you've brought a friend." She cast an approving glance and then offered her hand to Lord Carlyle.

Jocelyn released Carlyle's arm. "Lord Carlyle, this is Mrs. Harwood."

He executed an immaculate but somewhat stiff bow, one that looked as if he'd practiced it to perfection. There was definitely something different about Lord Carlyle. "Good evening, Mrs. Harwood."

Gertrude tittered. "Good evening, my lord. So charming! You *must* dance with Jocelyn!"

He cast a smile in Jocelyn's direction. "I plan to, ma'am."

Gertrude, and indeed all of her friends, sent congratulatory looks at Jocelyn. Just then, Jocelyn caught the sweep of a vivid blue skirt to her left. She turned her head and saw the woman wearing her mother's necklace approaching the terrace.

She pivoted toward Carlyle and smiled up at him. "I believe I'd like a bit of air first. My lord, would you mind taking me for a turn on the terrace?"

"Not at all." He looked to Gertrude and when she nodded

her approval, he offered his arm again.

Jocelyn strolled with him to the terrace, her feet moving perhaps a bit too quickly in her haste.

"In a hurry?" he asked.

"Sorry, I'm so short, I'm used to walking rapidly to keep up." It was the truth, but also provided a convenient excuse.

They stepped out onto the terrace. A few couples were enjoying the warm May air, including the woman in blue. Her companion turned at that moment, and his gaze fell on Carlyle. "Carlyle!" he called jovially. "I've been looking for you."

Jocelyn slid a glance at her escort. He knew those people?

Carlyle led her to the couple and performed another exemplary bow. "Lady Aldridge, you look lovely this evening."

She smiled at him and lifted a coy shoulder, which sent her dark ringlets swinging against her neck. "Carlyle, you are too kind. But then that's one of the reasons Aldridge and I adore you so."

Lady Aldridge squeezed the man's arm as she said the name, which meant he must be her husband. But he was at least two decades older than Lady Aldridge, who couldn't be more than a few years Jocelyn's senior. Indeed, at first glance, the man appeared to be Lady Aldridge's father.

"Lord and Lady Aldridge, allow me to present Miss Renwick. Miss Renwick, this is Lord and Lady Aldridge."

He *did* know them. Her estimation of Lord Carlyle dipped. Although she didn't know the circumstances behind Lady Aldridge's possession of her mother's necklace, Jocelyn couldn't help the outrage that washed over her every time she looked at the ivory pendant. She forced herself to relax and be rational. It wasn't Lord Carlyle's fault he was acquainted with people who were inexplicably in possession of stolen goods.

Lady Aldridge smiled, revealing even, white teeth and a dimple in her right cheek. She was very lovely. "Miss Renwick, how nice to make your acquaintance. Carlyle, I do believe you promised me a dance tonight, and I hear a new set starting."

Carlyle flicked a glance at Jocelyn, clearly looking for a way to claim their dance instead, but Jocelyn wanted the opportunity to question Lord Aldridge about her necklace.

She gave him a reassuring nod. "Go ahead. We'll dance the next."

Lady Aldridge's brow puckered as she turned her gaze to Jocelyn. "Truly, you don't mind? I haven't danced at all this evening. Aldridge's knees are paining him, you see."

Jocelyn hadn't danced in two years, but she bit back an unladylike retort and nodded her approval instead. "It's quite all right." She removed her hand from Lord Carlyle, who gave her another splendid bow and then led Lady Aldridge into the ballroom.

Armed with the wrath of the righteous, Jocelyn turned to face Lord Aldridge. Possessed of a light complexion and thinning gray hair, he was broad-shouldered and tall. But then everyone was tall to her.

She wasted no time launching her interrogation. "I encountered Lady Aldridge a few minutes ago and complimented her necklace. It's so unique. She said it was a gift from you. Do you mind telling me how you obtained it?"

He glanced to his left, toward the ballroom, before piercing her with an arrogant stare. "It's been in my family for generations."

Of all the pompous liars! Her heart thumped an erratic rhythm. "Indeed? It's exactly like a necklace that was stolen from my family two years ago. *Exactly*. Right down to the scratch in the glass. Are you quite certain of its origin?"

Aldridge glanced back toward the ballroom and then over his shoulder, as if ensuring no one could hear them. Then he stepped closer and spoke softly, but his eyes glinted dangerously. "You're mistaken, my dear. It's a family heirloom. I'm sorry for your loss, and I'm sure your necklace is somehow similar. Lady Aldridge's pendant, however, is not the same one." His tone was so patronizing, so *superior*, Jocelyn could only stare at him.

He started to move past her, but she did the unthinkable and grabbed his elbow. He turned a surprised glare on her. "I beg your pardon, Miss Renwick."

She let go of his sleeve, a bit shocked by her own cheek, but she was desperate. It simply wasn't possible the pendant had been in *his* family, not when she'd worn it at her very first ball!

"My apologies. However, you must understand how important this is to me. Is there any chance you purchased the necklace? Perhaps you've confused it with another piece?"

Aldridge's face reddened, and his forehead took on a sheen of perspiration. "I said you were mistaken, young lady. Do cease your impertinent questions."

His reaction told her far more than his words. He didn't like her inquiry at all and was discomfitted by it. Why? "My lord, I don't believe my questions are impertinent. Several valuable pieces of heirloom jewelry were stolen from my family two years ago. I merely wondered if you had perhaps purchased stolen property—unknowingly of course." She added the last when the flesh around his mouth paled.

"I assure you, Miss Renwick, I haven't purchased any stolen property—unknowingly or otherwise. Do you have any idea who I am?" He moved closer to her, which only served to make him tower over her like an ancient oak.

She squeezed her hands into tiny fists. He clearly believed her vulnerable to intimidation given her stature, but it was precisely because of her smallness that she refused to be bullied. "I'm afraid I've only just met you, my lord, so you must forgive my ignorance. I believed you to be the gentleman in possession of my late mother's necklace."

That did it. His nostrils flared and his lip curled. Fury rolled off him in waves. "I am not to be trifled with, gel. I do not take your insinuations kindly and advise you to desist any further pursuit of this topic."

And then he marched into the ballroom without a backward glance, mopping his forehead with a handkerchief from his pocket as he went.

Well, that had gone rather poorly. Jocelyn frowned after his retreating figure. She was as certain Lady Aldridge was wearing her mother's pendant as Lord Aldridge was that Jocelyn was mistaken. Was it possible he'd purchased a stolen item and was now too embarrassed to admit it? Perhaps, but he hadn't seemed embarrassed. He'd seemed furious and guilty, as if she'd caught him red-handed.

Jocelyn allowed the cool night breeze to soothe her temper.

At length, she returned to the corner of the ballroom Gertrude and her friends still inhabited.

"There you are," Gertrude said, her gaze searching the space around Jocelyn. "But where's Lord Carlyle?"

Jocelyn inclined her head toward the dance floor. "Dancing."

Gertrude's mouth dipped in disappointment. "I thought he was going to dance with you." Her gaze traveled past Jocelyn's shoulder, and her lips curved up. "The set is just ending. He's coming this way! Stand up straight, dear. Smile!" Gertrude assembled her expression into something a bit more sedate, but her eyes sparkled with excitement.

Jocelyn faced the dance floor, and indeed, Lord Carlyle was walking toward them. While she'd dearly love a dance, she wasn't sure she wanted to partner with someone who was on such friendly terms with the perfidious Lord Aldridge.

Carlyle arrived and gave a bow to Gertrude and her friends, who were lingering in the background. Then he directed the full intensity of his eyes upon her. And yes, intensity was the right word, for Lord Carlyle could probably look a hole clean through a person. Indeed, perhaps he could see through Aldridge's lies. "Are you still amenable for our dance?" he asked.

Her stomach gave a little flutter as she contemplated what else Carlyle might be able to see. "Yes." The acceptance slid from her lips before her brain had made up its mind. As they walked toward the dance floor, the strains of a waltz began, and Jocelyn was glad she'd agreed.

He took her waist and clasped her hand as he swept her into the music. His touch was light and gentle. Comforting.

Comforting?

She was not about to think of this gentleman as anything other than a potential adversary. Not given his acquaintances. Best to get to the bottom of that, then. "Lord Carlyle, how do you know Lord and Lady Aldridge?"

He turned his powerful gaze upon her again. Goodness, but she could stare at his eyes for an unseemly amount of time. She refocused on his shoulder.

"Perhaps you know I'm relatively new to Society?" he

asked. "I only inherited the viscountcy within the past few years. Before that I was, ah, not raised as a viscount's son. Lord Aldridge has been kind enough to help me adjust to my new role. Indeed, I don't know where I'd be today without his assistance and generosity."

Oh, dear. That was quite a bit more than acquaintances. "He's a close friend, then?"

"More like a relative, actually. I had a loving father, God rest his soul, but I suppose Lord Aldridge has behaved in that capacity for some time. Yes, I daresay he's been rather parental in his care and solicitation."

And with that, her *potential* adversary became her Adversary. How unfortunate, because she really could have lost herself in his eyes.

Chapter Two

DANIEL CARLYLE had struggled to participate in the game of courtship in London Society. Now that he had a title, he attracted simpering young women who sought to gain his name and newfound fortune. He'd yet to meet one with whom he could converse without cringing or whom he cared to actually court. Until Miss Renwick had stepped on his foot.

Instead of gasping in horror and bemoaning her clumsiness, she'd looked at him with curiosity as if wondering where he'd suddenly come from. She hadn't even apologized. And for that he considered dropping to his knee and proposing marriage immediately.

Her heart-shaped face was averted from him now, but he'd already memorized the delicate arch of her cheekbones, the saucy tilt of her nose, the luscious sweep of her lips, and the errant lock of light brown hair that nudged the perfect outer shell of her ear. But most of all, he wanted to see her intelligent hazel eyes look at him again with that curiosity that made him want to answer every question that tripped off her tongue. If he could. And if he couldn't, why he'd find the answer and deliver it to her on a silver platter.

Oh, for the love of God, he wasn't the least bit romantic, so what the hell was wrong with him? He gave himself an internal shake and promptly missed the dance step, nearly mashing *her* foot into the parquet.

"Sorry," he said, not for the first time annoyed with his lack of polish. Over two years he'd been studying how to be a viscount, and he still wasn't nearly good enough.

She glanced up at him, and he decided right then he'd step on her toes as many times as necessary to keep her spectacular gaze focused on him and not his shoulder or some object behind him. "It's quite all right," she murmured. And then she went back to looking into the distance.

She was a tiny thing; the top of her head barely reached the middle of his chest and her waist was incredibly narrow. He had the sense that his hand could span half the circumference, but of course he couldn't verify that without completely overstepping.

He searched for an appropriate compliment. "Miss Renwick, may I say you are lovelier than the flowers adorning this ballroom?" He tried not to visibly cringe at how inane that sounded.

Her gaze lifted once more, and Daniel couldn't help but smile, despite his lackluster flattery. He'd met dozens and dozens of marriageable females, but he'd yet to meet one that looked at him as she did. Like he was a full-blooded man with layers to unfold. Like he was more than just Lord Carlyle. Like he was simply Constable Daniel Carlyle again.

She blinked, fluttering ink-dark lashes. "And what flowers would those be, my lord? There are quite a few varieties in this ballroom."

Caught. "You've shamed me, Miss Renwick, for I can't name a single one." He'd been born and bred in London and had never taken the time to differentiate daisies from lilies.

"Not one?" she asked, her eyes widening. "You must know a rose when you see one?"

"I might, but I don't think there's one in this ballroom, so that doesn't help me. However, I *can* recognize a beauty far greater than a rose. Surely that is a superior skill," he countered, hoping he'd managed to turn a poetic phrase.

She laughed. Perhaps he'd been too hasty regarding his poeticism.

"You *are* new at this," she said, her eyes crinkling with amusement.

"Dreadfully." Despite his lack of refinement, he was thoroughly enjoying their exchange and hoped she was too. "You won't hold it against me, will you?"

She canted her head to the side. "That depends. Why don't you know anything about flowers? You have a country house, don't you?"

"Yes, in northwestern Essex." A two-hundred-acre estate he'd inherited with the title. But he'd spent the past two years learning how to manage the tenants and the various business interests of the previous viscount. Defining flower varieties had never once come up. "However, I employ a gardener." Or rather, the former viscount had employed one and so far, Daniel had seen no reason to replace any of the retainers. Indeed, he'd be quite lost without them. "I have to admit I'm more comfortable here in London."

"An inclination we share, my lord. I've only been to London a few times, but I am always saddened to return to Kent."

He was hoping for a bit more information about her situation. She wasn't married and was acting as a companion, yet wasn't old enough to be on the shelf—or so he surmised based on his limited experience in Society. He assumed she was without family, but didn't wish to pry if she wasn't of a mind to share. Perhaps he should share first. "My father would've learned the flowers. He would've made a far better viscount."

A pained expression flickered in her eyes. "How long ago did you lose your father?"

"Just over three years now." Edward Carlyle had been an excellent barrister and had been appointed magistrate at Marlborough Street. He'd been poised for an appointment in the Home Office when he'd suddenly taken ill and died. Yes, he would've filled the role of viscount with ease.

She gave a commiserative nod. "I lost mine two years ago."

They fell quiet as they turned about the dance floor. Daniel wanted to smooth the creases from her brow and coax her lips into a smile. Perhaps with his mouth…

"Why aren't you a very good viscount?" Her question saved him from pursuing lascivious thoughts, a thoroughly inappropriate endeavor in the center of a ballroom and proof yet again he was a terrible addition to the peerage. "What did you do before?"

"I was a constable in Queen Square."

Her head perked up. "The magistrate's office?"

He nodded. "I grew up exposed to the law. My father was a barrister, but instead of following in his footsteps I went directly to work for the magistrate."

Her eyes widened, and the curiosity burning there increased until they fairly sparked with excitement. "You caught criminals?"

"Yes." And he'd been good at it. While he appreciated the opportunity to promote police and prison reform from within the House of Lords, he missed chasing down a petty thief or hunting an embezzler.

"Like a Bow Street Runner?" She couldn't take her eyes off him now.

He stood straighter. "Much the same, yes." He couldn't discern the purpose of her unveiled interest. Did she romanticize the occupation? Some women did, and they were not women Daniel cared to know.

She gave him her full attention, and he couldn't detect a wistful quality to her gaze. On the contrary, she looked quite purposeful and serious. "Perhaps you can help me with a legal problem. Some of my family's treasures were stolen two years ago. Bow Street never found the thieves or the items. However, I've recently seen one of them and would like to have the person in possession of the item questioned."

Daniel tried to focus on the steps of the waltz as his blood surged with excitement. How he loved a good case to solve. But unfortunately that wasn't his occupation any longer. "You should visit Bow Street again and ask them to speak to this person. Or you could speak to a solicitor who could represent you in this matter. I would recommend my good friend Mr. Jeremy Bates."

Her eyes lit—they were so wonderfully expressive. "Thank you. I shall schedule an appointment with Mr. Bates at once." She paused, and her eyes darkened slightly. "Forgive me, but I'm a bit leery of approaching Bow Street. I don't believe they spent much time on our case, but then we had to leave London so quickly when my father fell ill after the robbery."

He couldn't help but think that if Queen Square had taken the case, they would've caught the thieves. "My apologies, Miss Renwick. That must have been a most difficult time. If I may be of any service in recovering your stolen property, I ask that you call upon me."

"Thank you, my lord. I may do just that."

He hoped so.

FOUR days later, Jocelyn sat in the office of Mr. Jeremy Bates, solicitor. Possessed of a kind countenance and a thick frame, he'd greeted her heartily and invited her to sit before his massive oak desk. He looked like someone who could protect you, which was precisely what Jocelyn wanted.

Seated behind his desk, he folded his hands atop a sheaf of papers, beside which was poised a pen and inkwell. He sat forward in his chair, prepared to listen intently. "How may I help you today, Miss Renwick?"

Jocelyn was pleased to have secured this appointment so quickly after Lord Carlyle had recommended Mr. Bates. Eager to share her problem, she too sat forward, clutching her reticule in her lap with both hands. "Two years ago, several of my family heirlooms were stolen from our town house. Bow Street was unable to recover the items or determine who stole them. They attributed the theft to one of the gangs of thieves who prey upon townhomes in Mayfair."

Mr. Bates nodded. "I'm familiar with such gangs. Go on."

"Several days ago I spotted one of the items—a pendant that belonged to my mother—on Lady Aldridge and when I asked Lord Aldridge where he obtained the necklace, he was rather rude and insisted—"

"Excuse me," Mr. Bates interrupted. "You questioned Lord Aldridge about this?" His tone was incredulous.

Jocelyn blinked at him, momentarily thrown by his reaction. "Yes. As I was saying, he insisted the pendant had been in *his* family, which is patently absurd."

"Wait." Mr. Bates held up his hand and then laid his palm flat against the top of his desk. "Isn't it possible you're mistaken about the necklace?"

Jocelyn expected this reaction and schooled her features to reflect a calm she didn't feel. The more she thought about the pendant—and she'd had plenty of opportunity over the past several days—the angrier she got. "I'm not at all mistaken. It's a singular piece, commissioned specifically by my father for my mother."

Mr. Bates frowned. His index finger began a rhythmic tap-tap-tap on his desktop. "He said it had been in his family?"

"That's correct. However, he's the one who's mistaken. I suggested he was confused, that perhaps he purchased the necklace without realizing it was stolen."

Mr. Bates's eyes widened. "You didn't."

"I most certainly did." She was beginning to grow annoyed with Mr. Bates's reactions. Yes, she'd questioned Lord Aldridge, and she didn't regret doing so. "That necklace belongs to *me*. I wore it at my debut ball. I should think I would recognize something I've seen in my mother's jewelry box my entire life." A box that had been left to her upon her mother's death nine years ago, when Jocelyn was just fourteen.

"I see." He gave her a sympathetic smile, then pressed his lips together. "However, you must understand, you can't simply go around accusing earls of harboring stolen property. Especially not Lord Aldridge."

She felt heat climbing her neck and worked to keep her temper in check. "Why not? He was defensive and became agitated when I asked him about the pendant. It was most suspicious."

Mr. Bates's fingertip stilled. "Why have you come to see me today?"

She loosened her grip on her reticule in an effort to ease some of her tension, but her back stayed ramrod straight. "I would like to recover my property. I want you to ask Lord Aldridge to return it, and if he refuses, I want to prosecute him for its theft."

Mr. Bates slowly leaned back in his chair. "Miss Renwick, have you any notion the trouble this could cause you, or the expense? No, I'm sure you do not, or you wouldn't have asked.

Lord Aldridge is an earl. Furthermore, he promotes police reform and seeks to eliminate crime in London. The idea that he would steal anything is absurd."

Jocelyn wasn't sure she could see Lord Aldridge behaving in an altruistic manner, but then her opinion of him was quite ruined due to his deceitful claim regarding the necklace. "Then I should think he'd be doubly pleased to see justice served. And since he's clearly in possession of stolen property, he should want to track down the thieves who stole it from me."

The solicitor gave his head a slight shake, and Jocelyn had the sense he was suffering her proposition rather than listening to her with an open mind. "Can you prove this item is yours?"

Triumph surged in her chest. "It bears a scratch in the glass covering the ivory. How could two identical pendants have the same defect?"

Mr. Bates's expression was patient, if a bit condescending. "I'm sure that seems like proof to you, but Aldridge could just as easily have damaged the pendant in his possession. You'd need something such as paperwork demonstrating ownership. Or perhaps a portrait of your mother wearing the piece. Anything that could provide *evidence* beyond simply your word that this pendant was in your family's possession prior to two years ago. Do you have anything like that?"

Jocelyn's elation ebbed as she searched her memory. There was nothing in writing and no portrait. A sick feeling spread out from her midsection, carving a hollow pit in her belly and making her shoulders slump. "No."

His eyes crinkled with sympathy. "I'm afraid there's nothing I can do to help you then. You see, this is a circumstance of your word against that of Lord Aldridge's, and I'm afraid since he's an earl … " His voice trailed off, but his unspoken words were obvious: Jocelyn had no chance against his title.

Outraged, Jocelyn recovered her rigid posture. "But that's my necklace!"

He averted his gaze from hers and shuffled the papers atop his desk. "Miss Renwick, if you could produce evidence that it belonged to you, we could try to recover the item. However, prosecution and a trial would be very expensive." He cleared his throat and looked back at her. "I hate to be indelicate, but do you have the funds for such a lengthy and involved legal procedure?"

She had very little funds, certainly not enough for what he was describing.

Mr. Bates's expression softened, and he gave her a kind smile. "I'm sorry I don't have better information to share."

She suddenly felt as if the theft had just happened. As if she and Papa had returned home to find their servants bound in the scullery and their rooms stripped of everything valuable. Her flesh turned cold as it had back then, as she'd crept up the staircase filled with stark fear at what she would find. At least they hadn't taken the actual jewelry box, only the half dozen pieces Mama had left her. And the watch fob Mama had given Papa, which he'd only left off that night because it had been in need of repair and he'd been afraid he might lose it.

Jocelyn swallowed the lump rising in her throat and stood. "Thank you for your time, Mr. Bates."

He also stood, his forehead creasing. "If circumstances change ... If you discover evidence and have the financial means, I invite you to contact me again."

She nodded, unable to summon even the meanest of smiles. Turning, she left the office and a few minutes later stepped into the bright afternoon. The sky was overcast, but the clouds were thin and high so that the sun's presence was still felt and seen. It was what her father had called the typical London spring day.

Papa. Her heart ached anew for his loss. He'd been utterly devastated by the theft of his late wife's belongings, and his beloved watch fob in particular. His health had apparently been poor for some time—a fact he'd kept from Jocelyn—and the crime had sent him into an attack of the heart from which he'd never recovered.

With heavy feet, Jocelyn set out toward Mayfair, where Gertrude had let a small town house for the Season. Her mind went over and over what Mr. Bates had told her. It couldn't be hopeless! That necklace was *hers*. She clenched her fists. There had to be a way to get it back! If not lawfully, why then she'd steal it back. Her steps slowed as the idea took on more substance than just an emotional reaction.

Could she steal it back? And do what with it? Wear it in public so Aldridge could call *her* a thief? No, she'd have to keep it hidden until she returned to Kent.

Yes. This could work. Her shoulders straightened. It *had* to, because it was, unfortunately, her only recourse. Though her insides still quivered, she had a sense of purpose. Of hope.

And perhaps just a bit of fear that she might get caught.

DANIEL spied Miss Renwick exiting the offices of his friend, Jeremy Bates. He'd hoped to encounter her at another ball or party, had even considered calling on her, but this chance meeting was quite an excellent turn of fortune.

He made his way to intercept her. "Good afternoon, Miss Renwick. What a pleasure to see you."

She tilted her face up. Her hazel gaze was direct and full of purpose. "Lord Carlyle, what a nice surprise."

He glanced behind her at his friend's office. "Were you visiting Mr. Bates?"

She nodded. "I was. Unfortunately, he was not able to help me."

He frowned, disappointed that the usually brilliant solicitor had somehow failed Miss Renwick. "I'm sorry to hear that. Perhaps I should have a word with him on your behalf."

She shook her head. "That won't be necessary."

"Will you at least allow me to accompany you to your destination?"

Her brow knitted very briefly, as if she were considering his offer and about to reject it. But then her lips spread into a full smile. "That would be lovely, thank you."

She laid her hand on his forearm. It was a simple touch, far more innocuous than their waltz the other night, but Daniel's entire body heated, starting at the very spot where her palm rested on his sleeve and spreading out to every part of him.

He forced himself to come up with an appropriate topic of conversation lest he dwell on her alluring scent. Apples. He knew his fruit, unlike flowers, and she smelled like apples. "Will you visit Bow Street next?"

"I don't think so. Mr. Bates gave me to believe my case may be hopeless. I can't produce evidence the stolen item belonged to me. It would be my word against the person who now possesses it, and I'm afraid I'm outranked." She shared the information calmly, but he detected an undercurrent in her tone and her hand tensed against his sleeve.

He was outraged on her behalf. "That's hardly fair."

"No, it's not, but what can I do? There are no living witnesses who can attest to the item belonging to me or my family, and I have no documentation or other proof the item was mine. *Is* mine." Her voice creaked with bitterness.

"Can I ask what the item is?"

"A necklace that belonged to my mother. It and a few other pieces that were also stolen were the only items I had of hers."

Daniel's own hands tensed. He longed to curl his fingers around the neck of the thief who'd stolen not just Miss Renwick's treasures, but the only tangible remnants she'd had of her mother.

She tipped her head up. "I wonder, my lord, if you might consider helping me in one area. You did offer assistance."

"Of course. I'd be delighted."

She smiled prettily. "I'd like for Mrs. Harwood to have a truly wonderful Season, and unfortunately our invitations have not been as plentiful as we might have hoped."

He saved her having to outright ask. The irony of *him* helping someone in this social fashion was rich, but he was glad he could do it for her. "I would be happy to secure some invitations for you and Mrs. Harwood."

"Just for Mrs. Harwood, really. I'm merely her companion."

He didn't think she was "merely" anything, but kept the opinion to himself for now. He was looking forward to courting Miss Renwick. And yes, he'd just decided to do that. A shock of anticipation shot through him. "Lord Aldridge is having a large dinner party tomorrow night. I'm certain Mrs. Harwood—and you—can be included."

Her eyes sparkled beneath the brim of her bonnet. "Thank you, my lord. I daresay that's perfect."

Chapter Three

DANIEL APPROACHED Lady Aldridge at her dinner party the following night. A charming young woman who'd been as helpful to him as her husband, she greeted Daniel with a smile. "Good evening, Carlyle," she said, extending her hand.

Daniel bowed and feathered a kiss on her gloved knuckles. "Good evening, my lady." He stood and stepped closer to her side. "I wanted to personally thank you for inviting Mrs. Harwood. Has she arrived?"

"Yes, she's in the drawing room, I believe. I'm happy to invite whomever you wish. You know you can count on me." She gave him a conspiratorial wink. "We may play some games after dinner. I'll make sure you and Miss Renwick are partnered together. That is why you had me invite Mrs. Harwood, isn't it? So Miss Renwick would be here?"

Lord Aldridge joined them at that moment, but his mouth was turned down as he looked at Daniel. "I feel it's my place to say you can do far better than Miss Renwick. Indeed, you *should* do better. You've a bright future, and you need a viscountess trained as the consummate hostess and Society wife."

Daniel's first instinct was to tell his patron to keep his opinions to himself, but as he'd spent the last two years soliciting the man's counsel, such a reaction seemed ungrateful. Instead, he slowly nodded once. "I see your point. However, I should like to make a match like yours and Lady Aldridge's. And, as you know, I've yet to meet a woman who has sparked my fancy."

Lady Aldridge gave him a knowing smile. "I've always thought you were a secret romantic."

Only since meeting Miss Renwick, which was at once terrible and exciting.

He was thankfully saved from commenting by Aldridge scoffing. "Don't encourage him in that direction. Miss Renwick is a nobody. I've invited Lord and Lady Winslow, and they've brought their daughter Lady Caroline." He looked to his wife. "You've seated her and Carlyle together for dinner as I instructed?"

"Of course. They're right next to each other."

He beamed at Lady Aldridge. "Excellent. Speaking of Lord Winslow, I must go and greet him." Aldridge looked to Daniel. "Come with me, Carlyle."

He should, and normally would have. But the pull of Miss Renwick in the drawing room was too much to resist. "I'll join you shortly."

Aldridge pursed his lips, but gave a nod and took himself off.

Lady Aldridge leaned in. "Never fear. I put Miss Renwick on your other side." She laughed softly and while Daniel appreciated her thoughtfulness, he was certain Aldridge would disapprove. Well, he'd leave that between them.

"Thank you, my lady. If you'll excuse me." He flashed her a smile, which she returned with a slight wave of her fingertips.

Daniel entered the drawing room a few moments later and immediately scanned for Miss Renwick. He suppressed a frown when she wasn't there. Her employer, Mrs. Harwood, was seated with another older woman, their heads bent in conversation. Disappointed, he turned and exited. He considered a moment before his feet took him to Aldridge's office—the place he felt most comfortable. He was still not quite at ease at these sorts of events, even after a year in Society.

Daniel recalled the day he'd learned of his inheritance as if it were yesterday. A solicitor had come into the magistrate's office in Queen Square and informed him of the death of his father's second cousin, Viscount Carlyle, *and* his son. That had been a year after his father's death and without his presence, Daniel hadn't a clue what to do next. Fortunately, the former viscount's secretary and valet, and the butler at Carlyle Hall, had turned out to be stalwart aides in educating him. He wouldn't say he'd mastered any of it, but he could at least muddle through his duties.

Aldridge had been the other integral piece of his training. They'd met at the Queen Street office when Aldridge, a proponent of police reform, had stopped in to talk with the constables on a few occasions. When he learned Daniel had inherited, he'd traveled to Essex to extend his sympathy and his assistance.

Daniel didn't know how he would've managed any of it without him. Every other nobleman he knew had been born and bred to their position, whereas Daniel hadn't known the first thing about his role in the House of Lords, how to manage his retainers, or how to acquit himself at a social event. Aldridge had, quite plainly, saved him from total humiliation and failure.

Daniel reached Aldridge's office and went inside. What greeted him made him stop in his tracks. "Miss Renwick?"

She stopped, her hand on the desk drawer she'd just closed. She stood straight and smoothed her skirt. Dots of pink colored her cheeks. She would have looked alluring if she hadn't also looked guilty. "Good evening, my lord. I do believe I'm in the wrong room."

Wishing to conduct his interview in private—and he intended to conduct an interview as the constable in him roared to the surface—he closed the door behind him. "What are you looking for in Lord Aldridge's office?"

"Nothing. As I said, I'm in the wrong place. I was looking for the retiring room." She moved around the desk and made for the door.

Daniel stepped into her path. "You thought the retiring room might be contained in the desk drawer?"

The pink in her cheeks darkened and spread. "Of course not. If you'll excuse me." She made to move past him, but he placed his hand on her forearm.

"I will not. At least not until you tell me what you were doing. You can't expect me to believe you were simply in the wrong room. You were looking for something. Tell me what it was."

She moved away from him as if his touch burned her.

Maybe it did. The feel of her skin beneath his palm was enough to heat him in the most inappropriate places.

"Please, my lord. I was mistaken. Just let me go." Then she dashed for the exit.

Daniel went after her, but she'd already opened the door and was stepping into the corridor. He stopped short lest he tackle her over the threshold, but then she spun on her heel and charged right back into him, sending him stumbling backward. She gained her balance, turned, and shut the door firmly.

Daniel lurched forward and, without thinking, pinned her against the door. He laid his palms on either side of her shoulders against the wood. "What the devil is going on?"

"Keep your voice down," she hissed. "Someone is in the corridor."

That's why she'd come right back into the office. He didn't move away from her. Instead, he enjoyed the heat of her body, the flush of her exertion, the shallow pant of her breath. She kept her eyes averted, but Daniel would get her to look at him soon enough.

"Unless you want me to open this door and let all and sundry see us together, you'll tell me what the hell you were doing in Lord Aldridge's office."

Her eyes snapped to his, their hazel depths flashing. She said, "You wouldn't," but her tone was laced with doubt.

He watched the muscle in her throat work as her pulse sped beneath her flesh, and her chest heaved. "You don't know me well enough to say for sure. Do you want to find out?"

She shook her head, her gaze never leaving his. He leaned a trifle closer until her breasts were almost touching his chest. Though she was petite, she was gently curved in all the right places. Her fresh apple scent assaulted him as surely as her proximity.

"Remember what I told you? About my stolen—"

Voices sounded outside, and Daniel instinctively put a finger to her lips. She'd kept her voice low, but only silence would do. How many times had he had to stop an informant from speaking so they wouldn't be overheard?

Her eyes widened. Was it because of the imminent danger

in the corridor or because he was touching her mouth? A number of illicit thoughts raced through his mind. Perhaps she was feeling the same.

After a few breathless moments, the voices faded. Daniel gently exhaled, letting his shoulders relax and his finger—regrettably—drop from her lips. He braced his hand against the door near her head, again caging her within his arms. "Your stolen property?"

She blinked at him as if she didn't remember who he was, let alone what they'd been speaking of. Then she gave her head a slight shake. "Yes," she whispered. "Lord—or I suppose Lady—Aldridge is the man in possession of my necklace."

She had to be mistaken. "Are you certain it's your necklace? Perhaps it's merely another one like it."

"*Just* like it?" She pursed her lips. "It's a one-of-a-kind pendant. Hand-painted on ivory."

"How can you be sure it's one of a kind?"

Frustrated lines etched across her forehead and around her mouth. "Because my father commissioned it from the artist specifically for my mother. It commemorated their first meeting, when he took her for a boat ride. Furthermore, it has a scratch in the glass—which *I* caused when I knocked it off Mama's dressing table."

That was pretty damned specific. Still, couldn't the artist have liked the piece so much that he'd duplicated it? And perhaps Lady Aldridge's necklace simply had a similar scratch. More likely, Aldridge had somehow purchased stolen property without knowing. Despite Miss Renwick's insistence and the apparent coincidences in the pendants, he found it impossible to think that Aldridge was involved in the theft of her items. More likely, he'd somehow unwittingly purchased stolen property.

She glared up at him. "Are you going to move away, or are we destined to be caught together in this office?"

Office ... Instead of retreating, he brought his face within an inch of hers. "What were you doing looking for a necklace in an office?"

Her head tipped back against the door, but she had nowhere to go. She swallowed, her gaze locked with his. "I wasn't looking for the necklace."

God, she smelled delicious. "What were you doing?"

Her breath hitched, and her pupils expanded. "Looking for something else."

"You'll have to be more forthcoming than that." He resisted the urge to press his mouth to her cheek, her throat, her parted lips.

"Evidence. I was looking for evidence that would prove Lord Aldridge is a thief."

She was playing a very dangerous game. Did she realize whom she was accusing? He lowered his right hand to just above her bare shoulder. With a feather-light touch, he brushed his thumb along the column of her neck. He was vastly overstepping propriety, but he didn't care. He'd been trained to use whatever skill and weaponry he possessed to take down a criminal, and right now she might be considered a criminal, regardless of her motivation.

"You won't find any. Aldridge is as law-abiding as winter nights are long. If he has your pendant, and"—he lowered his mouth to her ear—"I don't believe he does, he came by it honestly."

She turned her head and met his eyes with an angry stare. "He claims it's been in his family, but that's impossible. How obvious that you would take his position without even asking him."

"You can't go searching Aldridge's office. If you were caught—"

"I was," she ground out through gritted teeth.

"—by anyone other than me, you'd be ruined."

"If anyone catches me here *with* you, I'll be ruined. But, you see, I don't give a fig. I've no standing in Society whatsoever, no family, no plans to marry." She gave him a smug, daring smile. "There's nothing to ruin me for."

Daniel had been well versed in propriety during his recent education into the peerage, and she was quite mistaken. "There's Mrs. Harwood. Your behavior would reflect poorly on her."

Her color faded, and he felt a bit of sympathy for her. But it paled next to his need to kiss her. He curled his right hand around the side of her neck and gently pulled her toward him. Her lids lowered and her head tipped up to receive his kiss. Desire pooled in his belly.

But then her eyes widened, as if she'd just been doused with icy water. Her hand came up and pulled his away from her neck. "Go to the devil."

And then she turned abruptly and departed the office without so much as a glance into the corridor before she barreled straight into it.

Daniel watched the sway of her hips as she walked away. His ardor didn't cool. If anything it only fanned brighter, hotter. She was incomparable, that was for certain.

And since he'd heard the jingle of loose items in the pocket of her gown, he had to assume she was also, disappointingly, a thief.

Chapter Four

TWO DAYS later, Jocelyn strolled up Hertford Street after her usual early afternoon walk through Hyde Park. Her fingers went to the pocket of her gown where the three items she'd taken from Lady Aldridge's dressing chamber were nestled. Not only had she found her mother's pendant, she'd found two other items that had been stolen from their town house: a pair of pearl earrings and a brooch set with paste jewels. She'd been outraged upon finding them and hadn't thought twice about taking them back into her possession. They were, after all, *hers*.

Given that she'd found multiple items belonging to her family, she'd felt certain she'd find her father's watch fob amongst Lord Aldridge's things. However, she'd been unable to get to his dressing room. Disappointed but determined, she'd searched his office instead. Perhaps he kept records of things he'd purchased and she could prove these things *hadn't* been in his family as he'd previously claimed.

But then Lord Carlyle had found her.

Her pace slowed as she recalled the heat of his body as he'd pressed her against the door. He'd interrupted her search, and yet instead of remembering the jolt of fear, she flushed at the memory of the hint of clove that wafted from his collar, the intensity of his blue-gray eyes as he'd moved in for a kiss.

She pursed her lips and quickened her steps. Lord Carlyle might have been a potential suitor two years ago, but now he was nothing more than a nuisance. With any luck she'd be able to avoid him.

Except he was standing at the base of the steps leading up

to Mrs. Harwood's town house.

"Lord Carlyle," she blurted before she could order her thoughts.

"Miss Renwick. I've come to speak with you about the other night." His brows were drawn, his expression quite serious. He looked completely different from the first night they'd met, when he'd been all kindness and solicitation.

Her body tensed beneath his keen scrutiny. "I don't believe we have anything to say to one another, my lord. Please excuse me." She stepped around him and marched up to the door, but he followed.

When the door remained closed, Jocelyn frowned and then rapped on the wood.

"Where's your butler?" Lord Carlyle came up beside her.

If she hadn't been occupied with her concern, she would've told Carlyle to leave. "I'm not sure," she murmured, as the hair on the back of her neck stood up. She was recalling another time when the butler had failed to greet her …

"Allow me." He opened the door, pushing it wide so she could enter.

The small entry hall was deserted.

She stepped cautiously inside, her booted feet tapping against the marble tiles. "Moss?" she called.

No answer.

Carlyle followed her inside, and she was suddenly grateful for his persistent company. "Where would he be?"

Jocelyn chest constricted with oncoming panic. She tried to take a deep breath, to restore her nerves, but this was all too frighteningly familiar. "I don't know. Let's look in the—" She'd been about to say kitchen, but as they came abreast of the doorway leading to the front sitting room, she stopped short with a gasp. The room had been completely upset. A small writing desk was overturned, a vase lay in pieces, décor was strewn about as if every piece had been picked up and discarded without thought.

Oh God, it was precisely like two years ago.

"Stop." Carlyle's hand wrapped around her elbow and he drew her back into the entry hall. "Wait here."

She barely registered his words. Her eyes lost focus as her mind went back to when she and her father had returned home that disastrous April night. Their leased town house had looked the same. The butler had been trussed like a goose in the scullery along with the cook, housekeeper, and maid.

"Miss Renwick?" Carlyle's face came into view as if from a fog. "Miss Renwick." His tone grew more urgent.

She still couldn't draw a sufficient breath. Her chest rose and fell and her head grew light. "I ... I need to sit."

Carlyle guided her to the settee in the disordered sitting room. "I need to check on your retainers. Wait, is Mrs. Harwood at home?"

Jocelyn blinked up at him. Mrs. Harwood! Her heart skipped about her chest as if it wanted to break free and run, which is precisely what Jocelyn wanted to do. But she clutched the folds of her skirt instead. "I don't think so. She went to tea at Mrs. Montgrove's." Jocelyn prayed she was still there.

"How many retainers are there?"

"The butler—Moss, his wife—she's the housekeeper, and a maid. Look in the scullery first, please." She was torn between going with him and staying put. She didn't really care to be alone, but fear at what they might find below stairs froze her feet to the floor.

"You have to come with me," he said. "Until I can ascertain that whoever did this is no longer in the house, I want you by my side. Do you understand?" His eyes were clear, his tone utterly calm.

She nodded, unable to fault his logic. It was better that he made her decision, for she simply couldn't.

He helped her to her feet and he drew her close. "Take a deep breath, can you do that?"

Maybe. His hand drew circles on her lower back as she inhaled. Finally, air filled her lungs as he conferred his care upon her. She was still tense and scared, but for a moment, she found solace.

"Ready?" he asked, his touch gently slowing until stopping altogether. He kept his palm against her lower back.

"I think so." She told him the way to the scullery. They

crept down the stairs and near the bottom heard muffled sounds. Carlyle rushed forward and found the three retainers on the floor, their hands bound to each other behind their backs and rags tied around their mouths. They were trussed exactly as Jocelyn's servants had been two years ago. Shivers raced down her spine and up her arms.

Carlyle was already removing the rags from their mouths. The maid, Nan, began to swear, Mrs. Moss began to cry, while her husband thanked Carlyle profusely. Jocelyn jolted out of her shock, and she hurried forward to help untie them.

"Do you know if the culprits are still in the house?" Carlyle asked.

Moss shook his head while he massaged his wife's wrists. "I don't think so." He stood and helped Mrs. Moss to her feet.

Carlyle helped Nan up. "And Mrs. Harwood?"

"Still out," Moss said, "by the grace of God."

Jocelyn relaxed a bit at this news.

"Just the same, I think I'd better take a look around." Carlyle turned to Jocelyn and took her hands in his. "Stay here." He gave her fingers a squeeze and then raced up the stairs almost soundlessly.

While Carlyle was gone, they went into the kitchen and assembled themselves at the small table where the staff took their meals. Moss continued to hold his wife's hands and stroke her wrists in a soothing fashion. She kept looking into Moss's eyes and smiling tremulously, as if she were doing her best to reassure him.

Jocelyn blinked tears away. Their love and concern for one another was palpable and evoked bittersweet memories of her parents.

Nan made tea and when she'd set the pot to steeping, Carlyle came back down the stairs. All of them turned toward him with expectant eyes.

He took a seat at the head of the table. "The house is empty, but every room was searched. I can't tell if anything has been stolen."

Jocelyn was nearly certain nothing had, that what they'd wanted was tucked firmly in her pocket, but didn't say so. "I daresay we won't know until we clean up."

She laid her hand over her pocket, feeling the items concealed within. Relief that she'd decided to carry the treasures with her at all times joined her anger at what had been done to their retainers. She was only glad Gertrude hadn't been here.

Carlyle turned to Moss. "Can you tell me what happened?"

The butler gave his wife a reaffirming nod before turning his attention to Carlyle. "I answered the door, and they struck me in the head. The blow wasn't enough to put me out, but they easily overcame me, my lord." He sounded apologetic.

"You did fine, Moss. How many were there?" Carlyle asked, his tone warm and encouraging.

Moss looked a bit sheepish. "I'm not sure, my lord. Two of them dragged me down here, but it seems likely more came in after."

Nan nodded, her lip curling. "One came upstairs and found me. Tall bloke with longish blond hair. Nearly scared the life out of me. I tried to kick him, but he hauled me downstairs and handed me off to another one." She shook her head, muttering something unintelligible, and then went to get the tea.

"So perhaps four men?" Carlyle asked calmly. His demeanor didn't change—he wasn't agitated for angry, but resolute and logical. His skills as a constable hadn't diminished.

"We should notify Bow Street, shouldn't we?" Moss asked.

"Yes, but first I'd like to see if anything was taken." Carlyle focused his attention on Jocelyn. "Are you up to going through the house with me?" His stare was intent as usual, but carried a gleam of authority. He was in his element, solving a crime. She was going to have to tell him what she believed had happened, and he wasn't going to like it. Not when she'd committed a crime too.

She squared her shoulders. "Where do you want to start?"

"Your bedchamber, I think."

Jocelyn couldn't help the flush that crept up her cheeks. Was it inappropriate to allow a man into your bedchamber for the purposes of solving a crime?

She led him up the back stairs, climbing two flights to the first floor. At the threshold to her bedchamber, Jocelyn froze.

Her room hadn't just been searched. It had been destroyed. Her bed had been pulled apart and the pillows cut open. The drawers in the dresser set in the corner were all open, with the contents spilling out. Even the draperies on the window hung at an angle.

She stepped inside and moved into the tiny dressing chamber. This too had been ransacked. Her clothes lay strewn about the floor and, perhaps most telling, her mother's jewelry box was in pieces on the dressing table. And that made her furious.

"Is there anything missing?" Carlyle asked from behind her.

She went to the dressing table and picked up one of the shattered pieces of the jewelry box. Now was the time to tell him. She had to. After seeing him with the retainers, his concern for the entire situation, she wondered if he could help her. But would he? "I don't think so." She turned to face him. "I know what they were looking for."

The treasures in her pocket suddenly felt like lead weighing her down. She pulled them out and turned them over in her palm so he could see them clearly.

He stepped in front of her, staring at her hand. "You *did* take them."

She jerked her head up. "You knew?"

He raised his gaze to hers, but she couldn't discern what he was thinking—was he disappointed, angry, something else? "I suspected, which is why I came to see you today. I heard your pocket jangling when we left the office the other night, and when Lady Aldridge told me some things were missing from her jewelry box, I wondered if you'd taken them. Particularly when she said one of them was the pendant her husband had given her."

"It's *my* pendant. Just as these earrings and this brooch also belong to me."

He stared at her. "You stole them." His tone was still even, but beneath its deceptive calm seethed a current of anger.

He was angry then. She was getting there too. "I *recovered* them. It's not stealing if they're mine."

"You can't prove that—or so you told me. And you're mistaken. Lord Aldridge said the pendant wasn't yours."

She moved a bit closer as she glared up at him. "You don't find it rather coincidental that he has *three* items identical to mine? I might've been able to eventually accept the pendant was simply an exact version of my mother's, but not these earrings and the brooch too. No, these items belong to *me*." She curled her fingers around the jewelry in her hand. "Furthermore," she swept her hand out, indicating the devastation of her room," he doesn't want me to have them back."

His face was impassive, his eyes dark and devoid of emotion. "What were you doing in his study?"

He was well-versed in intimidation, but Jocelyn wasn't having it. She regretted using him for her own ends, but she didn't regret trying to uncover Aldridge's deceit. "Looking for proof that he'd either purchased these items or maybe ... something else. And there are other missing items, so I was looking for them." She lifted her chin.

His features froze and that undercurrent of fury spiked with fire in his eyes. "You manipulated me to secure you an invitation to Aldridge's house. You *used* me to commit theft."

He looked so furious, so ... betrayed that she couldn't help but feel a rush of shame. "I'm sorry" sounded so inadequate, but it was all she had. "I truly am sorry. I thought it was my only chance to recover my things. Please understand."

He glared at her another moment and then massaged his forehead. When he regarded her once more, his eyes had grown calm. His features relaxed into those of the helpful constable, making her wary. "You have to return the items," he said.

The hell she did. "I most certainly do not. I can't believe you'd even suggest it. What about him having Mrs. Harwood's house torn apart like this?"

His gaze drifted to the side, as he considered her question. "I can't believe Aldridge is behind your house being ransacked."

"Why not? He *had* to have been looking for these." She held up her closed fist. "He knows I took them."

His attention was focused on the wall as if there were something fascinating etched in the wallpaper. "Then he'd let Bow Street handle it." His voice trailed away.

"What? Why are you staring at the wall?"

Carlyle's gaze didn't waver. "Because he didn't tell me about the theft," he said quietly.

And of course he would have. They were close friends who championed police reform. This was a matter Lord Aldridge would've confided in Carlyle. Some of her anger leached away. "What are you thinking?"

"That none of this makes sense."

"Would it help to know this is precisely what happened two years ago when our property was stolen in the first place? Our retainers were bound together in the scullery, our house ruined." She couldn't keep the anguish inside. "It sent my father into a fit from which he never recovered."

At last, Carlyle turned his head toward her. "I'm sorry for your loss." He was quiet a moment. The space between them was scant, perhaps a hand's width. She could lean into him, seek his warmth, his comfort. But she didn't. He thought she was a thief, and she supposed she was. Did his opinion matter? She had no answer for that.

He pivoted away from her, creating distance between them, which was probably for the best. Whatever attraction she felt toward this man was doomed before she could even pursue it.

"You believe Lord Aldridge was behind the theft in your town house two years ago and what happened here today?"

She heard an edge of skepticism in his query, which made her want to raise her voice. But she didn't. She spoke calmly, if ironically. "I think it's suspicious that today's invasion looks exactly like the one two years ago, that it happened two days after I recovered some of my stolen property, and that Lord Aldridge hasn't reported his wife's missing jewels. You may draw your own conclusions, of course."

He arched a brow at her. "Thank you, I shall." He paced to the opposite corner of the small, square room. "I must agree it's all a bit suspicious. Lady Aldridge mentioned that her husband had advised her not to tell anyone about the missing jewelry, that she'd probably just misplaced the items."

"And is that typical for her?"

"Yes. She's been known to lose things now and again. She's quite reliant on her maid to keep things in order, and her maid has been gone the past week visiting her sick mother." He shook his head. "The more I think about this, the more I think you're batty. Lord Aldridge undoubtedly thinks his wife's jewels are somewhere in their town house, which makes perfect sense."

It would, if Lord Aldridge had told the truth about how he'd obtained Jocelyn's jewelry. "Except they're not in the Aldridges' town house, and someone ransacked this house looking for them."

He looked unconvinced. "You don't know that."

"I *do* know that." She picked through the clutter on the dressing table. "Nothing is missing. See, here—" She'd been about to say her silver earbobs were still there, but they weren't. And neither was the cameo Gertrude had loaned her the other day.

He came up beside her. "What is it?"

Her shoulders deflated. "My jewelry is missing." But how is it that the same thing could've happened to *her* twice? "I still don't think this is a coincidence. I think they came looking for these and took whatever else they wanted while they were at it."

"Have you considered an occupation as a constable?" he asked wryly and she turned to stare at him.

"How can you find humor in this situation?"

He exhaled and turned his body toward her. "I'm not. I'm merely saying you've a logical mind, if perhaps colored by your past experiences. Yes, it's coincidental that you've been robbed twice, but it's not impossible."

She spun to face him, still clutching her jewels. "How do you explain Lord Aldridge having three of my stolen pieces of jewelry?"

He shook his head, frowning. "I don't know, but I intend to find out. In the meantime, you have to return the items."

"I will not."

"Miss Renwick, surely you understand I cannot ignore a crime."

She was counting on it. "I do, and I'm asking you to solve mine. Do you believe these are my items?"

"I believe you think they are."

What a perfectly pompous thing to say. She put her empty

hand on her hip and gave him a direct stare. "Well, that's a bit insulting, isn't it?"

He sighed. "I don't think you're lying about them. There has to be a good explanation for the similarity."

She could work with that. "I agree. I propose you find that explanation—how these pieces came to be in Lord Aldridge's possession—and then I will return them, whether they were mine or not." How it pained her to even suggest they weren't hers, let alone return them!

He moved into her bedchamber. "All right. Let's start with a list of the things that were stolen from you two years ago. Can you write it down for me?"

"Certainly."

He turned toward her. "Excellent, please be as detailed as possible in your descriptions. While you do that, I'll ask Nan to make some order out of this room." His eyes flicked toward her ruined bed and then at her. She was suddenly very aware they were alone in her bedchamber. This thought was followed closely by the memory of his near-kiss the other night. A wave of heat assaulted her.

He focused his gaze on a spot on the wall behind her. Apparently the walls of her dressing room and bedchamber were riveting. He cleared his throat. "I'm going to send Moss for a constable from Bow Street."

It appeared his interest in her had waned. She tried to ignore her disappointment. "A Runner?"

His mouth turned down. "That's not what we're—*they're*—called. But yes."

She suspected he missed his former occupation more than a little bit. How shocking to go from being a constable to suddenly being a viscount without any choice in the matter. "Then we have a deal?"

His eyes connected with hers again and their usual intensity was heightened with a glimmer of excitement. Yes, he missed being a constable and he was eager for this task. Or, perhaps he wasn't as uninterested in her as she'd thought. "We do."

Despite the utter ruin of her bedchamber, Jocelyn felt hope for the first time in two years. She also felt the spark of something else, and it was something she'd never felt before.

Chapter Five

AFTER WALKING the Bow Street constable through Jocelyn's town house and ensuring everyone there was in good hands, Daniel had departed. He'd been a bit loath to leave her and her servants—Mrs. Moss was still quite agitated—but he'd done all he could without raising eyebrows, particularly because Mrs. Harwood had returned home. He told himself he merely wanted to see them all safe and secure, but he knew with Jocelyn it was a bit more than that. In her bedchamber, she'd looked at him with something akin to hunger. Then she'd glanced at her bed. He'd had to fight every male instinct he possessed to keep his hands and mouth to himself.

He caught a hack and directed it to St. Giles, where nearly all of his informants made their homes and conducted business, such as it were. His mind thrilled at the chance to solve a crime again. He could scarcely wait to speak with his favorite fence, assuming Odette was still operating her flash house. If she wasn't, it meant she'd come to a tragic end, because he couldn't see the shameless former prostitute ever leaving her livelihood.

One of the problems he'd come up against as a constable was the differing views regarding treatment of certain criminals. Was Odette breaking the law as a fence? Absolutely. And once, as a green constable, he'd attempted to arrest her, until he'd realized that in prison she wouldn't be able to help him catch bigger villains. So they'd begun a mutually beneficial relationship in which Daniel ignored her fencing activities—within reason—and she provided him with information that led him to snare a large number of thieves.

The hack stopped in front of the Silver Unicorn. He paid his driver and inhaled the familiar filth of the rookery. He didn't miss *that*, but the scent went hand-in-hand with fighting crime and that made him smile with anticipation.

Odette's flash house hadn't changed in the years since he'd been gone. The sign still bore a prancing white, not silver, unicorn. Four dogs loitered at the entrance and Daniel recognized the largest, a scruffy gray mongrel with huge brown eyes. "Gray," he greeted, using the animal's none-too-original moniker. "How've you been, boy?"

Gray remembered Daniel too, for he nuzzled his hand and his tongue lolled from his mouth. Daniel spent a minute petting the dog and then had to extend the kindness to his furry friends who'd come looking for attention.

With a final pat to Gray's head, he turned toward the interior. Gray gave his hand a lick and Daniel smiled, reminded of his dogs at home. Rather, the pair of hounds he'd inherited at Carlyle Hall in Essex. When had he started to think of that as home? He shook the thought from his head and focused on the task before him.

The taproom of the Silver Unicorn was as low-ceilinged and dim as he recalled. At this time of day, the place was empty, which made it his favorite time to visit. He walked to the back, where the bar stood, its scarred surface bearing witness to the years it had been in existence.

A dark head popped up and froze at the sight of him. "Danny Carlyle!" Odette exclaimed. At just past middle age, Odette was still a comely woman, if a bit brash in her looks. Her forehead was just a bit too wide, but was forgiven by a pair of sultry eyes with lashes as thick as pitch. And the tip of her nose was too blunt, but the lush curve of her lips drew one's attention immediately south.

She raced around the bar and threw her arms around his neck. They'd never been intimate—she was old enough to be his mother—but Daniel often thought she'd wished she were younger.

He hugged her in return and when she finally let him go, he stood back and, with mock sincerity, said, "Don't you mean

Lord Carlyle?"

"Oh, good Christ! You don't expect me to curtsey and simper, do you?" She curled her lip in distaste, but quickly smiled. Then she sank into an energetic, if not perfect, curtsey. "My lord, to what do I owe the pleasure of your visit this afternoon?"

He pulled her to stand. "You can knock that off and pull me a pint." Odette served some of the best ale in London.

"As my lord instructs." She laughed as she sauntered back around the bar.

Daniel leaned against the wood, his eye finding the gouge in the middle where he'd dodged a knife one night. His blood heated at the memory. Could he still hold his own in a fight?

She slid his ale across the bar and gave him a mock scowl—he could tell by the twinkle in her eyes. "It took you long enough to visit me."

"My apologies, Odette. It turns out being a viscount is harder than being a constable."

Her boisterous laugh filled the room. "What rot." She pulled herself a pint of ale. "As much as I adore you, I'm sure you didn't come to ask after my health. Though, it would've been nice if you had."

Yes, it would have. "I am appropriately chastised. I shall endeavor to do better. I wonder what Society would say about me frequenting a flash house in St. Giles?"

She chuckled. "That you're a wastrel or a drunk. Or both."

He took a long draught of ale. The flavor reminded him of countless nights in establishments just like this, asking questions just like this one: "How's business?"

She put her elbows on the bar and folded her forearms in front of her. "Same as usual."

"I was hoping you'd say that."

"Liar, you were always hoping I'd narrow my focus." Give up the fencing, she meant. Though she was dead helpful, he liked her and worried for her safety. Too many fences lost their lives over a dispute or dissatisfied customer.

"I'm hoping you can help me with something that would've happened two years ago. Several items were stolen from a friend of mine." He'd convinced Jocelyn to give him the items so he could make inquiries. Rather than pull all three from his pocket, he withdrew just the pendant, since it was the most distinctive of the pieces. He laid it atop the bar. "Do you recognize this?"

She pulled a lantern closer and leaned over to inspect the necklace. Her weathered fingers smoothed the glass that covered the ivory. "Lovely. But I haven't seen it before."

Daniel had so been hoping she could help him. Her specialty was trafficking items stolen from the homes of the wealthy and privileged. "Think back, if you can. The item was stolen from a town house in Mayfair. There were multiple pieces. A brooch, earrings, a watch fob that was also hand-painted." He removed the other items from his pocket. "Here."

She looked up at him, her brow arched. "Withholding from me, eh?"

He tipped his head in apology.

She picked up the brooch and studied the paste jewels. "Where's the watch fob?"

"It hasn't been recovered."

After discarding the brooch, she studied the earrings. "Where'd you find these?"

"Doesn't matter."

She withdrew from the jewelry and assumed her previous position with her arms folded on the bar. "It does if you want answers. You know how this works, Danny."

Yes, he did. Information begat information. "They were found in the house of an earl. I believe he bought them without realizing they were stolen." It was the only reasonable explanation. Aldridge had lied about them being in his family to save face. If word got out that he'd purchased stolen items, his reputation as a crime reformer would be ruined. Furthermore, Daniel simply couldn't believe he was guilty of more than that.

Odette's head perked up. "An earl, you say?"

Daniel leaned forward, his pulse quickening at the lure of information. "Yes?"

"Don't know anything about that." She took a drink of ale.

Daniel suppressed a frown. It was best to keep all emotion out of these sorts of discussions. It was never helpful to give anything away, something Odette was trying her damnedest not to do. But he saw through her denial. Whenever she didn't have an answer for him, she always offered to find out. Why not this time?

"Can you ask around for me?" he asked. "But try not to say it's an earl. I'd prefer to keep the gentleman's identity secret."

She scoffed. "There's a thousand earls or summat, aren't there? Sure, I'll see what I can find out, but given how long ago this happened, I wouldn't expect much. Your friend should just be happy to have her things back."

He reached out to pick up the jewelry, but laid his hand over hers instead. He looked at her intently. "I'd really like to know who stole these. There are other items she'd like to find, things that are particularly valuable to no one but her."

Odette's face softened, and she turned her hand over so they were palm to palm. "You always were a bit sentimental. Find yourself a wife yet? Maybe this 'friend' of yours?"

Wife? He'd planned to court Jocelyn before she'd turned to thievery. He was definitely attracted to her, but could he overlook what she'd done?

He scooped Jocelyn's—when had he begun to think of them as hers?—jewels into his pocket and ignored the wife questions. "I'm not sentimental. You're just a hardened criminal."

"Shhh! You're not supposed to say that out loud."

He flashed her a smile. "Afraid the rats might turn you in?"

She laughed loudly again. "Get yourself gone, Danny Carlyle—sorry, *my lord*," she drawled outrageously.

"You can send word to me here." He gave her one of his cards.

She took the card with one hand, and with the other put her index finger to the tip of her nose and pushed it up. "Brook Street. Fancy-pants."

He took another pull from his ale and set it back atop the bar. Then he dropped several coins next to the battered glass. "Thank you, Odette. Take care of yourself."

"Good to see you, Danny," she said as he turned and departed her establishment.

He was disappointed in her lack of information, but intrigued by what she didn't say. Still, he didn't doubt she'd find a way to be of help. She'd use the errand boys who lodged in her rafters to go fact-finding, and Daniel would employ a few boys to do the same.

As he made his way further into the rookery, he considered whether he should speak to Aldridge. But what could he say? Aldridge would demand the return of the jewelry, and Daniel would have to abandon his inquiry. When he approached Aldridge, he had to do it armed with facts.

Jocelyn's jewelry weighted his coat pocket. Yes, when *had* he begun to think of these items as her property? He realized then that he did believe her, not just that she thought the items were hers, but that they had indeed been stolen. He recalled the fear in her eyes, the tension in her body, the panic in her voice when they'd gone into her town house that afternoon. To have that happen once was bad enough, but twice? And she'd yet to break under the distress. She deserved to know what had happened, and he was going to find out.

Chapter Six

THE FOLLOWING afternoon, Jocelyn surveyed her mostly-tidied bedchamber. It had taken the rest of yesterday and the better part of today to clean up the feathers from the bedding and remove the ruined linens and mattress. It would be several days before the bedding could be replaced. In the meantime, she was moving into the spare bedroom, which was smaller and sported a lumpy mattress.

Moss appeared in the doorway. "Miss Renwick, Lord Carlyle is here to see you."

Her stomach did a little flip. Just when she'd despaired, confident of a future on the shelf, he'd walked into her path—literally. And now, hope warmed her breast.

She stepped down the stairs with a jaunty bounce. Daniel—oh, she mustn't first-name him, but what was the harm if she did so privately?—was waiting for her in the entry hall, his hat in his hand.

He smiled as his gaze lit on her, and her stomach flipped again. "Good afternoon, Miss Renwick." Such an address sounded so formal after what they'd been through together yesterday. She was so glad he'd come upon her when he did. If she'd had to face the ruined house alone ... she shuddered.

His eyes crinkled with concern, and he stepped toward the stairs as she reached the last step. "What's wrong?"

She gave him a bright smile. "Nothing. I was just thinking how happy I am you were with me yesterday."

His features relaxed. "I'm happy too—and relieved you were not at home when the invasion occurred." He paused, smiling at her in return. "I was hoping you might like to take a turn around the park with me. I have a phaeton, though I have to confess that while I've mastered riding, I've yet to truly grasp the finer points of driving."

He was so honest, so matter-of-fact, that she couldn't help but continue to smile. She'd never met a more self-aware person. "I'm sure you're better than you think. And good for you for mastering riding. That's no easy feat."

He nodded, his lips turning up at her compliment. "Thank you. The head groom at Carlyle Hall said I was a natural. I think he was trying to ensure I didn't sack him. All the retainers tiptoed around me for a good three months before they realized I was more afraid of them than they could possibly be of me."

She picked up her bonnet, which she'd worn earlier on her walk, from a table in the foyer. "You weren't really afraid?"

He bowed forward as if he were imparting a deep secret. "Terrified. I'd had a cook, a housekeeper, and a butler who served as my father's valet for a time, but the number of servants at Carlyle Hall was positively intimidating. They knew everything I didn't, their manners put mine to shame, and I daresay a few of them might've been garbed better."

She tied the ribbons beneath her chin and pulled on her gloves, also from the table. "I don't believe that for a minute."

He looked at her with mock incredulity. "Have you seen the amount of starch in the shirt of a butler who's in charge of a large manor house? It could stiffen the Thames."

She laughed and then informed Moss of her departure. Daniel held the door open for her and escorted her to his phaeton, a sleek, black lacquered affair with a gorgeous bay.

She walked to the vehicle and ran her hand along the side. "Your vehicle is splendid. But if you aren't comfortable driving it, why do you have it?"

He came up beside her. "Because I inherited it, and Aldridge assured me it was the height of fashion for me to drive a phaeton. Do you think I could do without it?"

The mention of Aldridge was like a dark storm cloud, but Jocelyn refused to let the vile man dampen what was turning out to be an outstanding afternoon. She pretended his name had never been invoked. And since he'd advised Daniel to keep the phaeton, she was contrary enough to suggest just the opposite. Plus, it was true. "Anyone who would judge a man by his vehicle is no one worth knowing. Such opinions are asinine. I wouldn't care if you drove a twenty-year-old barouche." She purposely let her gaze turn serious. "I wouldn't care if you drove nothing at all."

He helped her up into the phaeton, and his hand lingered around hers. "You just demonstrated the value of your opinion. I shall rethink the phaeton." His eyes connected with hers on an intimate level, confirming the mutual admiration growing between them.

He gave her hand a squeeze before releasing it. Warmed by his attention, she slid across the seat—but not all the way to the other side—as he climbed up to sit beside her.

"I'd forgotten how high up we would be," she said, eyeing the faraway ground. She hoped he was a better driver than he said.

With a flick of the reins, he smoothly guided them forward. Though they weren't touching, he sat close enough to her right side that she could feel his heat. "You've ridden in a phaeton before?" he asked.

"Just once, during my Season." She studied his profile. He was distinctively attractive. "I tried to recollect you from then, but I can't."

"That's because I wasn't in London two years ago. I inherited the title a few months prior and wasn't ready for Society yet." He gave her a conspiratorial smile. "Though I'm still not sure I am."

He was too hard on himself. At least he didn't go around with a mouth that overtook his brain. "Nonsense. You're equal to the task, my lord."

He stopped the phaeton before turning onto Park Lane. "I appreciate your confidence. Though it's been a challenge. People assume that because I was a constable who wasn't raised to be a peer, that I'm somehow … less."

She understood the prejudice he faced. "Which is ludicrous because you've likely done more good than most of them could imagine."

He cast her a sideways glance, his dark eyes burning bright beneath the brim of his hat. "You're doing wonderful things for my self-esteem."

"Somehow I doubt it's in much danger. Still, I applaud you muddling through in the face of everyone's judgment. Society can be quite terrifying in their assumptions." She studied him from her side of the phaeton. "What would your assumptions have been of me? If you made them, which I'm sure you have not."

He guided the phaeton along Piccadilly toward Hyde Park Corner. "On the contrary, I made a very wrong assumption when I first saw you across the ballroom on the night we met. I immediately supposed you must be married. A beautiful young woman like you had to be."

His words sent a delicious heat across her skin. "You saw me across the ballroom?"

The look he cast at her took her breath away. "Why do you think you stepped on my foot? I'd moved to intercept you."

The heat dove inward, and awareness sparked inside of her. "I'm afraid I wasn't paying much attention."

"I remember. You were barreling across the ballroom as if your life depended on it."

Following Lady Aldridge. "I'm afraid when I've set my mind to something, I'm rather single-minded. I don't always see everything I should, such as your foot."

He chuckled. "I understand. I'm the same with a case. My father used to say I could be consumed by my work if I wasn't careful."

"And was he right?"

"Yes. It's probably good I stopped to become a viscount." He nodded very slightly as if he were responding to some inner conversation she couldn't hear. "Working so closely with criminals takes a toll."

His words elicited a dark shiver along her neck. They turned into the park, which was crowded with vehicles and pedestrians since it was nearing five o'clock.

"Is it wise of you to be working on my case, then?" she

asked.

"I think so. It's just one case after all. But I may be out of practice. I haven't anything to report as of yet, I'm afraid."

She laughed, hoping to put him at ease. He wasn't really disappointed in his abilities, was he? "It's only been a day!"

"Yes, but I'm used to quick results." He smiled lopsidedly. "I told you I could get lost in my work."

She was fascinated by his experience. He was so different from every other gentleman she'd met. "Will you tell me about it?"

He slowed the phaeton, not that they'd been going overly fast, and joined the park traffic. "It's not terribly exciting."

She tapped his sleeve with her palm. "Don't bam me. You want to talk about it."

He grinned at her. "Investigative work involves talking to a lot of people. As a constable, I amassed a great number of contacts. I've visited some of them, but so far none have had any useful information. I'm hopeful that will change. I have boys making some inquiries and following—never mind, this must be dreadfully dull."

"Not at all, I find it intriguing." *If only because it's about you.* She wanted to know everything about him, how he'd diverted from a potentially troublesome occupation to embracing his title. Wait, did he embrace it? "You say it's good that you became a viscount. Do you really think so? You've said you're not very good at it, but from what I can tell you're better than average. You dance well, your driving is excellent, and you're far more entertaining to talk to than any of the gentlemen I met during my Season."

"And were there a lot of gentlemen?" He slid her an inquiring glance, and she briefly wondered if he were jealous. If she thought about him talking with other ladies ... She was suddenly *quite* jealous.

"Not so many. I was only out a fortnight before the robbery." She didn't want to think about that. This was the best day she could remember in such a long time. Maybe forever.

He turned his head toward her and she felt the weight of his stare like a caress. "I'm glad." He hastened to add, "About the number of gentlemen, not the robbery."

"Of course."

"I should be sorry your Season ended that way, but selfishly I'm glad it means you're here now. With me."

Her pulse picked up with anticipation. "My lord, are you hoping to court me?"

His blue-gray eyes were intent, captivating. "I might be. Would you be amenable?"

While she'd enjoyed their flirtation immensely, she had to know if he was earnest. She didn't want to get her hopes up for nothing. "I'm surprised by it, my lord. I thought my stealing my possessions from Lord Aldridge rather put you off."

His hands tightened around the reins, making Jocelyn think of her own stretched nerves as she waited for his response.

"I'll be honest, it did. But I also understand why you did it. Your willingness to return the items if Lord Aldridge innocently purchased them is honorable, and I respect you for it."

Her chest lightened. "Thank you. Though it will be quite difficult to return them because they *are* mine," she said, half trying to provoke him. However, his attention was focused on a gentleman standing at the left edge of the path: Lord Aldridge.

She squared her shoulders and steeled herself against his odious presence. She really had nothing but loathing for the man because she didn't think for a moment he could possibly be innocent.

"Carlyle!" Aldridge called. His gaze flicked to Jocelyn, and she didn't miss the deep lines that spread out from his mouth before he forced a smile. "Miss Renwick."

Daniel steered the phaeton to the left and came to a halt beside Aldridge. "Lovely day," Daniel said. "Where is Lady Aldridge?"

Aldridge inclined his head to a grassy area off the path. "Chatting with her friends."

The earl stood perhaps ten feet away, close enough for Jocelyn to wish she was on the other side of the carriage. Her eye was drawn to his lavender waistcoat. It was a rather feminine color, and then she noticed the ribbon of his watch fob matched the hue. And there, dangling at the end of the ribbon, was her father's hand-painted fob. She leaned so far forward to get a closer look that she almost fell out of the phaeton.

Daniel's hand came around her waist and he pulled her back into her seat. If she wasn't so agitated by the sight of Papa's fob on that scurrilous Lord Aldridge, she would have appreciated the intimacy of his rescue. Instead, she said, "I couldn't help but notice your fob, my lord. What a unique piece." As unique as her mother's pendant.

Aldridge slid his fingers down the ribbon and stroked his thumb over the glass-encased, hand-painted ivory oval that was so similar to the pendant. "It is indeed."

"I simply must know where you got—"

Daniel's hand squeezed her waist, which sent a ticklish jolt up her side. She jumped and turned to look at him. He gave her a dark, meaningful stare that said, "Hold your tongue." Which was a constant battle for her. With great effort, she closed her mouth and smiled with a serenity she didn't feel.

Aldridge's brows lifted, but then he schooled his features into a benign expression. "Good to see you, Carlyle. I'll see you at White's later?"

"Probably. Give my best to Lady Aldridge." Daniel guided the phaeton back into traffic. When they were several yards away, he said, "You can't speak to Aldridge like that, especially in public." He kept his voice low, but the disapproval in his tone was as loud as church bells.

She turned slightly in her seat so she could see him better. "I can't ask him a simple question, yet he can rudely say it was "good to see you" without addressing my presence?"

Daniel threw her an exasperated glance. "What did you expect him to do after your behavior?"

"*My* behavior? You're the one who manhandled me in public."

"I had to do something before you spoke completely out of turn. Careful, or next time I may find another way to occupy your lips." He pinned her with a hot, penetrating look.

It was perhaps the only thing he could've said to shut her up. And it worked perfectly. Jocelyn sat back in her seat and stared forward while heat collected in her belly. Next time. *He'd* better be careful or she'd make it her life's work to publicly interrogate Aldridge. A kiss—public or otherwise—from Daniel would be worth any price.

She slid a glance at his mouth. It was very nice, with a plump lower lip that she suddenly imagined nibbling with her teeth. Good heavens, she wasn't a wanton, what was wrong with her? She'd hoped to find someone, but to feel this level of attraction was a surprise. A very welcome and heady surprise.

He turned the phaeton down another path toward the Grosvenor Gate. It seemed their drive was nearly over. She regretted her overzealous tongue. Had she put him off entirely? She snuck another look in his direction and started when she realized that his eyes were fixed on her like a cat stalking a bird. But unlike that bird, she had no wish to fly away.

"Where will you be this evening?" he asked, his raw voice—it lacked the cultured specificity of most London fops, she finally realized—spreading over her like cream on a hot scone.

"At home." She stared at him, unable to look away from his magnetic gaze. "Mrs. Harwood doesn't like to go out every night."

He blinked, lessening the spell between them, but not breaking it entirely. "Pity, for then I can't ask you to dance again."

She nearly exhaled with relief. She hadn't lost him, then. If he could tolerate her runaway tongue, she might have to marry him on the spot. Provided he asked her, that was. As usual, she was getting ahead of herself.

"Tomorrow we'll be at the Pellinghams'," she said.

"Excellent, I shall be sure to be there as well. In the meantime, I will continue my investigation and keep you apprised of any developments."

"Thank you."

They fell silent again as they left the park. When they turned into Hertford Street she found the courage—which in itself was noteworthy, for she never had to strive to speak—to ask, "Did you mean what you said earlier? About occupying my lips?"

He stopped the phaeton in front of her town house. "I not only meant it, I'll consider it a disappointment if I don't get the chance."

Chapter Seven

WITH NO hope of seeing Jocelyn tonight—he vaguely noted he'd somehow switched to thinking of her by her Christian name—and a half-promise to meet Aldridge at White's, Daniel made his way up the steps of the St. James Street club. It had been such an invigorating afternoon, even with her faux pas. He was already counting the minutes until their dance. And maybe something more.

Damn, but being a viscount certainly made things difficult. In his old life, he would've been able to steal a kiss—or more—by now. He supposed he could've yesterday at her town house. However, the timing had been extremely poor. He wasn't the sort of man who kissed someone after her house had been robbed.

A footman opened the door, and Daniel made his way inside. The interior was filled with important, wealthy, privileged men. Men with whom Daniel barely felt comfortable. Being here at White's, amidst all of the history and pomp, had been very intimidating at first, but now it was just ... necessary. If he wanted to be an influential member in the House of Lords, he needed to participate in all the trappings of being a lord. It wasn't that he didn't enjoy the political discussions he often engaged in here, particularly when he was able to bend someone's ear about the need for police reform or the deplorable conditions in London's prisons, especially the "hulks" bobbing in the Thames, carrying thousands of prisoners in their filthy depths. No, it was everything else that taxed his patience—the betting book, the gambling, the excessive drinking. He'd seen enough of that behavior during his constable days and he'd seen it executed by far better sots than these pretenders.

Aldridge hailed him from a table on the other side of the room. Daniel made his way toward the man who'd been such a good friend and confidant the past two years. He never could've navigated the breach from constable to viscount without his help. And now he had to accept the possibility that the man could be a criminal. He gave his head a mental shake. No, that couldn't be possible. Aldridge might've had no knowledge the items had been stolen. At worst, he'd purchased stolen property, and he'd refused to acknowledge it to Jocelyn because he was embarrassed to have been caught.

But what of the watch fob he'd been wearing today? If he were truly embarrassed, Daniel would think he'd either return the fob to Jocelyn or at least hide it away. Instead, he'd worn it quite blatantly.

"Carlyle, I've ordered our usual." A bottle of ten-year-old Highland whisky sat in the middle of the table. Aldridge poured him a tumbler. "Good to see you."

Daniel sat and accepted the glass. "Thank you." He took a swig, savoring the smoky tang as it slid down his throat. He never could've afforded such luxury as a constable. Peerage definitely had its benefits.

Aldridge sipped his whisky. "You know I've always guided you well, don't you?"

"Of course, and I appreciate your help."

Aldridge nodded vigorously. "Certainly, my boy, certainly. There's no easy way to say this, so forgive my candor. Miss Renwick would be a perfectly acceptable wife if you were Constable Daniel Carlyle. However, you're now Viscount Carlyle, peer of the realm. You should set your sights much higher. You *need* to."

It came as no surprise that Aldridge would want to steer him away from Jocelyn. If matters did progress with her, he hadn't the foggiest notion how things would go with the earl. And he didn't want to have to choose one over the other. Although, if Aldridge were somehow involved in the theft of Jocelyn's things, or if he refused to recognize they were rightfully hers, Daniel was going to have a difficult time maintaining their friendship.

He set his glass on the table, but kept his fingers curled around the base. "Does it really matter who I marry, provided she isn't a pariah?"

"Absolutely," Aldridge said, his eyes full of fiery conviction. "It's of the utmost importance. You need a wife who can manage your households, preside over social events, and make dukes feel comfortable."

"You don't know whether Miss Renwick can or can't do any of those things." Neither did Daniel, but he suspected she could—and well.

Aldridge leaned forward, his forearms braced on the table as he cradled his glass of whisky between his hands. "Here's what I do know: During her Season two years ago, she was immediately marked as Trouble. With an impertinent mouth and flirtatious nature, she quickly gained a reputation as a ... loose female."

She did all that in a fortnight? Daniel had expected Aldridge to disdain his growing interest in Jocelyn, but he hadn't been prepared for all-out warfare. "I have to think you're exaggerating," he said softly, but with an edge.

Aldridge set his glass down and gestured with his hands, as he was wont to do when he was engaged in a conversation he cared deeply about. "I'm only telling you the truth. If you marry her, many will think less of you for it, and it will be difficult for you to effect the change you want. I know how committed you are to creating a true police force, and how much you care about improving the conditions of our prisons. Are you prepared to abandon those endeavors for a woman whose virtue may or may not be pure?"

Daniel's hackles rose, and he gripped the whisky glass like a weapon. "Careful. I won't have you impugn an innocent's reputation."

"Carlyle, how well do you know this girl? You've only just met. I have it on good authority she was in London looking for a husband because she'd been thrown over by someone in Kent. Someone with whom she'd already been intimate."

Outrage on her behalf threatened to spill forth from his mouth, but he kept himself in order. With a composure he didn't feel, he took a healthy drink of his whisky. When the fire reached his belly, he allowed the warmth to calm his rising temper. "How could you know such a thing?"

"Lady Margaret Rutherford has infallible information about everybody."

Lady Margaret was the most feared gossip in London and perhaps all of England. A spinster with a supposed network of informants that would likely rival his own, her *on-dit*s were generally accepted as truth, even if the majority of them bordered on the malicious.

Aldridge plucked up his whisky and downed the remainder. Then he reached for the bottle and poured another glass. "I'm only asking you to listen to my counsel. We've known each other awhile now, and I only have your best interests at heart. I should hate for you to ignore my advice—which is coming purely from my concern for your welfare—and suffer the consequences."

Daniel couldn't ignore the man's earnest plea. He did know the earl far better than he knew Jocelyn. And he had to admit she did have an impertinent tongue. He'd seen evidence of it just that afternoon. Could the rest be true? He doubted it. And more importantly, it was of no consequence, at least not to him. However, he also recognized he couldn't be the viscount he wanted to be if he married someone who would be scorned. Furthermore, he *had* caught her stealing. It didn't matter that she'd been taking items she believed were hers, she'd bent the law in her favor.

His insides twisted. Hadn't he bent the law on countless occasions? He knew Odette and his other informants were criminals, could have sought their arrest on any given day. But he hadn't. He'd accepted that he had to allow a little wrong to do a lot of right. How was that different from her actions?

"My lord?" A footman arrived at their table, breaking into Daniel's internal discussion. "I have an urgent note for you." He handed Daniel a folded parchment.

With a frown, Daniel accepted the paper from the footman's gloved hand. "Thank you."

He unfolded the missive and read the hastily written lines:

Please come at once.
Jocelyn

He stood quickly, nearly knocking his chair over. Jocelyn might not be the right viscountess, but he already felt more strongly about her than he had any other woman. "Please excuse me."

Aldridge got to his feet as well. "What's wrong? May I be of assistance?"

"No, I have to go. I'll take your counsel into account." His heart pounded, and his muscles grew tense and tight. It was all he could do to walk sedately from the club.

JOCELYN paced the small entry hall waiting for Daniel to arrive. Her thoughts went from what she'd found upstairs to the encounter with Aldridge at the park to the delightful flirtation she'd shared with Daniel. Her blood warmed at the thought of seeing him tonight, and for that reason alone she was glad she'd found the clue.

A sharp rap drew her from her reverie. She rushed to the door and opened it wide.

Light from the entrance hall illuminated Daniel's face—his dark blue gray eyes, his strong, square chin, and that bottom lip she still wanted to nibble.

He immediately crossed the threshold and closed the door behind him. "Where's Moss?" His voice was filled with alarm.

The smile forming on her lips died upon hearing his concern. "In the kitchen with Mrs. Moss. I told him I'd answer the door."

He frowned down at her. "Do you think that's wise, given what happened here? I don't want you doing that again."

That he cared so much for her welfare warmed her to her very soul. Her smile crept back. "I won't. I promise."

"But you're all right?" He put his hands on her shoulders and grazed them down her arms to her elbows, which he clasped gently.

His touch made her move closer to him. "I'm fine."

He frowned again. "Your note could've said so. I was worried."

Oh, dear. She'd dashed that note off without thinking. She should've added that she'd found a clue. But his solicitude felt so nice, she was perversely glad she hadn't. "I'm sorry. Next time I'll be clear." She grinned up at him. "I've found a clue! Come!"

She turned and, without thinking, took his hand to lead him up the stairs. When he didn't follow, she stopped and turned back. He was staring at their joined hands. Then he seemed to come back to himself and stepped toward the stairs. Stifling a happy smile, she took him upstairs to her former bedchamber.

He paused again at the threshold and, disappointingly, dropped her hand. "Where is Mrs. Harwood?"

Jocelyn moved inside, but he remained at the door. "Abed already." Was he hesitating because of propriety? "Come in and see, I found a knife under the bed."

Daniel hastened to join her and knelt at the end of the four-poster where she stood.

She lowered herself to kneel beside him. "I came to remove the last of my things to my new chamber, and I saw a flash beneath the bed. It was the blade of a knife."

He reached under the bed and pulled the weapon into the light of the lantern she'd set on the dresser. He stood, and she moved up next to him in order to see the weapon. The blade was maybe six inches, but the handle was the truly remarkable part. It was in the shape of a dragon with red-jeweled eyes and had a tail that curved to form a rounded hilt.

"It's so unusual," she said. "I questioned the servants after I found it. Nan said she was in here tidying when the thieves came in and hauled her downstairs. She believes one of them may have dropped it."

Daniel frowned at the weapon. "I recognize this knife. It belongs to a man I arrested several years ago, Nicky Blue. I'll go and see him at once." He turned as if he really meant *at once*.

She rushed around him and blocked his exit. "Wait! Where are you going? May I accompany you?"

His brow furrowed, and his gaze had turned quite dark. "St. Giles, and hell no. Pardon my language. It's not an appropriate place for a lady, especially at this hour."

St. Giles? Even she knew that was one of the worst places in all of London. "I shall worry for your safety."

His features softened a bit, but he diverted his gaze from hers. "Don't, I'm quite comfortable there and no one will bother me. They know I'm a constable—or was a constable."

Yes, there was definitely something wrong tonight. And being who she was, she couldn't simply let it go. "Are you still angry with me about what I said to Lord Aldridge earlier? I'm sorry, but it was just so jarring to see my father's watch fob on his person. Particularly when he knows I know he had my things."

"No, I'm not angry." His eyes found hers again, and she could see that he was telling the truth. He wasn't angry, but he was *something*.

"Will this knife help me get my fob back?"

"Perhaps." Daniel took her hand—maybe he was all right after all—and said, "Don't worry. I'm not going to let anyone bother you again. Bow Street is keeping an eye on your house."

She clasped her fingers around his, wanting to keep him with her for as long as she could. Bow Street was fine, but he was better. "They are?"

"Yes."

"Thank you." She moved a bit closer to him and placed her other hand on his upper arm. "I don't know what I would have done if I hadn't met you. It's been so long since anyone has sought to take care of me." Then she knew she couldn't let him go without the kiss that had been simmering between them since yesterday.

She stood on her toes and watched him watch her. His eyes were dark, unreadable. Then she closed her eyes and pressed her lips to his. He was soft and warm, and desire flashed through her, bright and hot.

She laid her hand atop his shoulder and opened her eyes. His gaze was still dark, but his lids had lowered, giving him a rich, seductive look. Her pulse quickened.

"Jocelyn," he breathed. It wasn't a question, but a warning, as if he were trying to stop himself.

But she didn't want him to.

She curled her hand around the back of his neck and tilted her head to the side. Closing her eyes once more, she kissed him again.

This time, his hands came around her waist and he hauled her up against his chest. His lips moved over hers with insistent pressure. Where he'd let her kiss him the first time, this was him taking control. She clutched at his head as if her life depended on it, and maybe it did. She'd never felt such delicious sensation, such heat swirling through every part of her. The contact of his chest against her breasts was new but so exciting. She wondered how it would feel with nothing between them.

Then he completely distracted her thoughts by sliding his tongue along the crease of her mouth. She opened instinctively, and he swept inside. Oh. This … She was dumbstruck. He was all heat and velvet and bliss. Thank God he was supporting her weight; otherwise she would've melted into the floor.

His tongue caressed her mouth, coaxing her to join him in the dance. Tentatively, she touched her tongue to his. He brought her into his mouth, showing her how to kiss him back as thoroughly and divinely as he was kissing her. She never imagined it could be so lovely. So enchanting.

So *perfect*.

His hand stroked up her spine and cupped the back of her neck and then her head. With his other hand, he cupped her hip and pressed her pelvis against him. Because of the difference in their height, she felt the hardness of his arousal against her belly. She arched higher on her toes, trying to fit herself to him to appease the need that had blossomed between her thighs.

His mouth slid from hers, and he languished kisses along her cheek and then down her neck. She dropped her head back as his lips worked a path to her collarbone. His hand glided upward from her hip along her ribcage until it met the underside of her breast. It was as if the contact awakened every sensation inside of her. Her breasts grew sensitive, and they tingled with anticipation. She wanted more.

Thankfully, he gave it to her. His hand cupped her breast. Then his thumb dragged over her nipple. Despite the layers of clothing keeping her flesh from his, she felt his touch as if they were skin to skin. Suddenly his mouth was at the top of her bodice. He was pushing the top of her breast up and over the edge of her gown while his mouth suckled her flesh. She couldn't keep a moan from escaping. When had she become an utter wanton?

Then his mouth stilled, and his hold on the back of her neck loosened. Since he was supporting less of her, she came back down onto her feet, which created a cold distance between them. She opened her eyes and looked up at him in bewilderment.

"Why did you stop?" She sounded as breathless and aroused as she felt.

He made sure she was standing straight without assistance, then took a step back. He pressed his fingers to his mouth. God, did he regret kissing her? No! She didn't want that. She moved forward, but he only retreated another step. His eyes were focused low and to the right of her and his mouth was pulled down at the corners. Lush corners she wanted to kiss again and again.

"I have to go," he said, turning.

"Daniel, wait." She grabbed his elbow, not caring how her actions appeared. "I don't want you to go."

He looked at her then, but his eyes were unreadable. "You must agree I have to. I'll let you know what I learn from the knife. Good night." And then he was gone from her.

Jocelyn stared at the open doorway for several minutes while her body and emotions cooled. Why had he pulled away at that moment? He'd been enjoying their embrace as much as she. Even more, she believed they at least liked each other very much. In truth, she might even feel a bit more strongly than that.

Dejectedly, she readjusted her bodice. Then she made her way to her new bedchamber with leaden feet.

Chapter Eight

INSIDE THE hired hack on the way to St. Giles, Daniel called himself every insult he could think of. What the hell had he been thinking, kissing her like that? She wasn't some woman he visited in a flash house or a widow he tarried with after sharing an ale at the neighborhood pub. She was Miss Renwick. An estimable, virtuous young woman from a good family.

But now he had to wonder if she was what Aldridge purported her to be.

He could scarcely credit what Aldridge had said at White's, but then she'd kissed him. Then he'd gotten quite carried away, and she'd allowed it. His confidence about her was more than shaken.

Nevertheless, he spent the entire trip reliving her kiss: the taste of her mouth, the feel of her body, the sound of her moan. It was all he could do not to release his cock from his drawers and finish the job they'd started.

Instead, he tried to focus on his journey into St. Giles, a rookery so foul and so corrupt that no sane police officer ever entered it at night. Unless they'd spent years cultivating mutually beneficial relationships, which Daniel had done.

However, he'd made no such affiliation with Nicky Blue, who was as vile and unlawful as they came. It had given Daniel great satisfaction to see the man locked away, if only for a short time. He doubted Nicky would be helpful, but Daniel hoped the return of his prized knife would make him at least slightly amenable. Daniel would also make it clear he wasn't after Nicky—unless Nicky had acted alone. Making such a promise would turn Daniel's stomach, but it was the sort of accord that would allow him to snare the prize he wanted. In this case, that was whoever was behind the theft of Jocelyn's things.

It was nearly eleven of the clock, which meant Nicky ought to be at a flash house drinking and either eyeing a mark or waiting for a later hour to launch whatever misdeed he had plotted. The question was which flash house. Daniel would start at the outer edge of St. Giles and work his way inward.

Nearly two hours later, he'd been to six establishments and hadn't yet found his quarry. But he wasn't frustrated. Such was the life of a constable on the hunt. Except he wasn't a constable anymore.

What the hell was he doing, hunting down thieves?

Helping someone he cared about.

He realized then that he cared about Jocelyn. Perhaps she'd permitted—even invited—far more to happen tonight than a typical young lady would or should have, but he'd been glad for it. How was a man with his background supposed to get on with a simpering Society girl?

Which maybe made them a perfect match. A match he had to admit he wanted. He could see himself marrying her, was beginning to think of it seriously, in fact. He liked her fiery spirit—even her impertinent tongue—and her intelligence. That she was a warm-blooded woman unafraid to embrace her own desires only made her more attractive. Furthermore, he wanted to trust her. She'd been honest with him about taking her jewels from Lord Aldridge, and Daniel could see she'd only done it because she believed there was no other way. She'd consulted with a solicitor to try to solve the problem lawfully and when that had failed, she'd become desperate. Plus, her willingness to return the items if Daniel found that Aldridge had legally purchased them illustrated the goodness of her heart. A heart that was likely better than his own.

He made his way further into the rookery. Now and again he saw a familiar face, but more often strangers looked at him as if he were a sheep for slaughter. Outfitted in the richer trappings of a viscount instead of his former, plainer wardrobe, he likely seemed an easy mark for the denizens of St. Giles. They'd be in for a surprise if they tried to rob him. He'd have the knife out of his boot and against their throat in a trice.

He stepped into the next flash house on his mental list, the Crystal. Decorated with sparkling lanterns and flowered wallpaper, it aimed to attract wealthy, daring gentlemen out for a night of depravity in the "gutter." He'd seen Nicky Blue here a time or two, but more importantly he'd seen some of Nicky's associates and perhaps they'd be willing to help run him to ground—for a price, of course.

The interior was crowded with gaming tables, mostly filled at this hour. Women were sprinkled about, all of them hawking their wares, but in a more subtle fashion than those on the street. Daniel scanned the room and looked for a familiar face. He stopped when he reached the far back corner. Sconces on the wall illuminated a table with five men sitting around it. One had his back to the corner and was clearly holding court: Ethan Jagger.

Daniel made his way to the corner, the knife in his boot a welcome weight as he approached one of the highest-ranking criminals in London. Jagger was one of Gin Jimmy's right-hand men, overseeing a large number of operations from thievery to fraud.

Jagger was roughly the same age as Daniel, maybe slightly younger, which was notable given his status. But then he'd been on the streets almost half his life—or so Daniel had gathered after many years of investigating Gin Jimmy's sergeants—and had worked hard to achieve his rank. With jet-black hair and piercing gray eyes, Jagger was as cold and harsh as they came, but he also possessed an intelligence that would rival any barrister or official Daniel had met. It was too bad the criminal had taken the path he had. From what Daniel knew, his life could've been vastly different.

"If it isn't Mr. Carlyle," Jagger drawled. His brow arched, and he sat forward in his chair. "No! You're *Lord* Carlyle now, aren't you? What the devil are you doing in St. Giles?"

"Mind if I sit?" Daniel asked, grasping the back of a chair.

"Not at all. Whisky?" Jagger picked up the bottle in front of him and reached for an empty glass. The Crystal prided itself on fancy glass tumblers that were supposed to be reminiscent of the gentlemen's clubs in St. James.

"No gin?" Daniel preferred whisky, but gin, due to its quantity, was usually the drink of choice in St. Giles.

"Not at my table. I've taken to drinking whisky of late." Jagger poured him a glass, and one of his henchmen slid it across the table to Daniel.

Daniel glanced around the table and held up his glass in mock toast before taking a healthy swallow. "It's quite good. From your personal supply?"

The corner of Jagger's mouth hitched up. "Of course."

Daniel set his glass back on the table. "May we speak privately?"

"Certainly." Jagger nodded at the other four men around the table. They stood and departed without a word.

Jagger leaned back in his chair so that his head rested against the wall. "What do you want to know?"

It made sense that Jagger would assume he was here for information. The only other kind of help he provided was financial in nature, and Daniel would never want to owe money to the likes of him.

Though he despised sitting with his back to the door, Daniel knew Jagger would see his vulnerability as an expression of confidence. He expected Jagger to have his back, and because of that, Jagger would. So Daniel settled into his chair. "I'm looking for Nicky Blue."

Jagger sipped his whisky. He kept the glass cradled in his palm as he addressed Daniel. "I haven't seen him tonight."

"Can you tell me where to find him? Or, better yet," Daniel withdrew the knife from his coat pocket and set it atop the table so Jagger could see it, "can you tell me how I came to find his weapon under a bed in a house in Mayfair?"

Daniel hadn't shown the knife at any of the other flash houses, but he was certain Jagger would recognize the distinctive piece. The question was whether Daniel could get the criminal to work with him, or if he'd claim he'd never seen it.

Jagger barely glanced at the blade. "Maybe because Nicky was shagging a Society widow?" He laughed, then sobered when

Daniel didn't laugh with him. "No sense of humor tonight? How dull. Why would I know what his knife was doing in Mayfair?"

"Because you oversee Nicky's crew." Daniel sat forward slightly. "Let's not play games. I'm not a constable anymore. I'm trying to help a friend find some things that were stolen from her two years ago."

Lifting his shoulder, Jagger maintained his aloof expression. "That's very kind of you to help someone in need, but I fail to see why *I* should care."

Daniel eyed the man in his rich costume that was paid for by criminal activity. Like his cohorts, Jagger dressed to intimidate, but unlike them he wasn't garish. Except for the two rings he wore on each hand—which was excessive by fashionable standards—he looked as if he could be in any Mayfair ballroom. Indeed, if he were so inclined, he could probably march right into one tonight and claim his place. "Because deep down you might like to help someone too. Have you forgotten I know who you really are? Where you come from?"

Jagger suddenly snapped to attention, his eyes hardening. "What's more important is that you don't forget who I am now." He stared at Daniel, letting the threat stand for a long moment.

"Because I am a trifle more benevolent than most, and because I can appreciate wanting to help a young woman," he cast him a knowing glance, "I'll tell you that Nicky targets houses in Mayfair."

Daniel had figured as much and opened his mouth to say so, but Jagger held up a hand. "Don't interrupt," he said, "I'm not finished. His targets are always successful because he knows precisely where to strike."

Suddenly Daniel understood. Nicky Blue had a man—or woman—on the inside. "He has intelligence on where to go and when."

Jagger gave a single nod, then scanned the room behind Daniel, something a criminal like him always did as a means of defense.

"I don't suppose you'd tell me who?"

Jagger blinked innocently. "Who what?"

Right. "If I give you a name and I'm correct, just remain silent." Daniel's neck muscles bunched with anxiety. He dreaded the answer, but he had to know. "Aldridge."

Jagger slowly brought his whisky glass to his lips and took a long drink, his eyes never leaving Daniel's.

Damn. Aldridge had clearly at least purchased stolen goods, but to be part of the actual theft? Daniel's stomach briefly clenched in disbelief before anger wiped away all other emotion. The earl had been his friend, his mentor. They'd plotted together on how to improve the city's police. Daniel had shared so many things about his life as a constable—how much of that information had Aldridge used to further his own criminal interests? And how in the hell had he gotten mixed up in all of this in the first place?

"I'll expect something in return," Jagger said, drawing Daniel's attention from his inner turmoil.

He wasn't surprised Jagger would want something. It was the way things worked. How many times had Daniel been forced to turn his head in exchange for the greater good—ignoring smaller crimes so that he could go after bigger ones? "What do you want?"

Jagger lifted a shoulder as he again surveyed the room behind Daniel. "I'm not certain yet, but I'll let you know."

"Just remember, I'm not a constable anymore."

Jagger smiled blandly. "I'm well aware of that."

Daniel decided it was time to invoke a bit of the constable still left in him. He laid his palm flat on the table and speared Jagger with his most intimidating stare. "How does Aldridge communicate his information? Tell me that, and I'll do whatever you need." God, how he hated making such promises, but if it meant he could take down Aldridge, he'd do it.

Jagger's eyes lit with merriment. "You always had an excellent reputation here. I see Society hasn't softened your instincts. To answer your question, he sends a coded note. I'll see that you get the information contained in the next one. But I'll need that knife to coax Nicky to let me see it."

Daniel's blood surged with victory. "It's yours." He tossed back the rest of his whisky and stood. "Thank you for the drink."

"Out of curiosity, who's the woman? I imagine she must be worth quite a lot to you if you're willing to dip your toes back into this sordid life."

Daniel nearly laughed. As if he'd tell him. Jagger had a reputation for using people to reach his own ends. "Thank you again."

Jagger's eyes gleamed devilishly. "It's all right. You know I can learn anything I desire."

Every shred of Daniel's good humor fled in the face of his sudden fury. Jocelyn had been victimized, and he'd be damned if he let Jagger even speak her name. He stepped around the table, closer to Jagger, and glared down at him. "If I hear so much as a syllable of her name from your lips, or see you or any of your associates in her proximity, I'll not only forget I ever agreed to help you, I'll make it my life's goal to see you hang." He let his threat gather momentum, just as Jagger had done. Then he bared his teeth in a vicious smile. "Given all you've done, I don't think it will be too difficult." He exhaled and straightened his coat, though it didn't require adjustment. "I look forward to hearing from you."

Then he turned and stalked from the flash house, his back prickling slightly under the stares of Jagger's henchmen, who'd approached the table as soon as Daniel had moved toward their boss.

Outside, he made his way out of the rookery. He'd planned to attend a ball, but he didn't want to run the risk of seeing Aldridge. Such an encounter could prove quite detrimental to the man who'd played Daniel for a fool.

He suddenly wanted to go directly to Jocelyn's house so he could tell her what he'd learned. He'd also apologize for pulling away and beg her forgiveness for listening to even an iota of Aldridge's lies. Then he'd take her in his arms and finish what she'd started ...

But no, he wouldn't do that. It was quite late, and she deserved a real courtship with a real proposal of marriage. His step lightened as he considered how he might ask her.

Chapter Nine

THE FOLLOWING afternoon as Jocelyn was reviewing Mrs. Harwood's invitations in the upstairs sitting room, Moss interrupted to tell her she had a guest: Lord Aldridge.

"I've shown him to the front sitting room, Miss Renwick," Moss said.

Her insides clenched upon hearing Lord Aldridge was here, but she was glad for the opportunity to put him on notice: Very soon he'd have to return the watch fob and why not do it now?

She rose from the desk. "Thank you, Moss."

As she descended the stairs, she wondered why she hadn't heard from Daniel yet. Given the way he'd left last night, she almost wondered if she'd ever hear from him again. Papa had always said her mouth would get her into trouble if she wasn't careful, but she'd never imagined it would be because she'd kissed someone. She still inwardly cringed when she thought of her daring and Daniel's subsequent departure.

She entered the sitting room to find Aldridge standing near the fireplace, his forehead creased and his mouth drawn into a pinched frown.

"Miss Renwick." He said her name without an ounce of pleasantry. Indeed, it sounded rather like an epithet.

Jocelyn's shoulders bunched up as tension coiled through her frame. "My lord."

"I've come to discuss your ridiculous allegations regarding my property, as well as your scandalous relationship with Lord Carlyle."

Scandalous? Oh no, what had Daniel told him? She worked to keep from blushing of embarrassment and instead focused on the first thing the earl had said. "We both know it's *my* property, including the watch fob you were wearing yesterday. It belonged to my father."

He flushed scarlet and his eyes narrowed. "You are a pest, do you know that, Miss Renwick? Like a rat that continues to invade one's scullery."

Jocelyn was rendered momentarily speechless, which was quite a feat. She found her anger—and her tongue—and said, "Insult me all you like. We both know you stole my things. And more importantly, Daniel knows it too." She tried to bite back the words. She hadn't meant to reveal Daniel's support, but the earl's rudeness had provoked her reckless tongue. Again. She tried not to cringe.

Aldridge strode across the sitting room and closed the door. A chill snaked down Jocelyn's spine. He stalked toward her, stopping just in front of her. "What precisely did you tell him?" he asked softly.

She notched up her chin, looking for the courage that had suddenly ebbed from her frame. "That you saw fit to have our town house ransacked the other day."

He didn't look the least perturbed by her revelation, merely cocked his head to the side. "If he's mounting evidence against anyone, I'd beware; it might be you. That's why I came here today. Carlyle is fully aware of how I obtained these items. He's the one who put me in touch with the fence who sold them to me."

Jocelyn gaped at his smug smile. It couldn't be true. Daniel had wanted to help her, certainly not implicate her. He'd seemed so excited last night when she'd given him the knife. But he hadn't sent any news since then. And there was the troubling way he'd retreated from their embrace. A bead of doubt wedged itself into her mind and took hold.

The earl's mouth remained curved up in that nauseating smile, and his eyes glinted with glee. "Carlyle has kept all of his old contacts. I know he maintains a relationship with at least one fence—a woman named Odette who owns a flash house in St. Giles."

"Relationship"? What sort of relationship? Was that why he'd pulled away from her last night? Jocelyn felt sick. All she could think to say was, "Daniel was a constable."

"And like so many of our police force, he's corrupt." He shook his head and held up his palm while lifting his shoulder. "It's simply the way of things, gel."

Jocelyn's knees weakened, but she refused to show her disappointment. She couldn't believe Daniel would do anything Aldridge was saying, but how well did she really know him? Not at all, she realized.

"Now, if I were you, I'd take myself back to my little village in Kent and forget about all of this nonsense. I'm feeling benevolent enough to give you the watch fob. I always found it a trifle mundane for my taste, anyway." He withdrew the treasure from his pocket, and she thrust out her hand to accept it. When the weight filled her palm, she closed her fingers around it and just barely kept herself from punching Aldridge in the face with it.

"I'd also advise you not to mention this conversation to anyone, especially Carlyle. Those who have proposed his behavior is less than lawful have sometimes disappeared."

What on earth was he suggesting now? That Daniel murdered people? Or had them imprisoned? She simply couldn't credit it. "You expect me to believe he's that cold?"

Aldridge shrugged. "Believe what you like. However, if you tell him what I told you, he'll deny it." He leaned forward and added, "And then you'd better watch your back."

She took a step back. "Are you threatening me?"

"No, I'm helping you make an informed decision regarding what you do next. I suggest you stay as far away from me and 'Daniel' as possible."

Her mind swarmed with everything Aldridge had told her. Daniel was corrupt? He was compiling evidence to implicate her as a thief? He'd ensure she "disappeared" if she revealed what Aldridge had told her? She didn't want to believe any of it.

It was not lost on her that Aldridge would benefit from her keeping silent and leaving London. But how much did she really know about Daniel?

She tucked the watch fob into her pocket with fingers that shook more than she wanted. "Thank you for returning my property, my lord. Now, if you'll excuse me."

She gestured to the door, indicating he should leave. But he didn't. Instead, he moved close enough that she could see the pores on his face.

"Don't be foolish, Miss Renwick," he said in a low, sinister voice." I hope you'll heed my advice." She stepped back, and her hands involuntarily came up in a defensive posture. His lip curled before he spun around and quit first the sitting room and then the town house.

Jocelyn let out the breath she'd apparently been holding, and most of the tension left her body. It was time to find out once and for all if Daniel was the monster Aldridge described or the man she was falling in love with.

TODAY had not gone as planned. Daniel had intended to visit Jocelyn early this afternoon to propose marriage, an endeavor he'd delightfully orchestrated last night during his walk back to the Silver Unicorn, where he'd meant to catch a hack. However, a brawl inside Odette's establishment had drawn him into the flash house.

A gang of older boys had become quite unruly, and Daniel's inner constable hadn't been able to walk away. Trying to instill peace, he'd ended up getting dragged into the fight. Ultimately, two officers had arrived, and together they'd put an end to the disturbance. Some of the lads had been carted off to Newgate, while the others had dispersed. It had been dawn before Daniel finally returned to his home and fallen into bed. Now it was midafternoon, and he was scrambling to get to Jocelyn's.

At last, he was making his way downstairs when he heard his butler talking with someone in the foyer. He turned onto the landing and saw Jocelyn standing in the middle of his marble floor. Garbed in a pale yellow dress with an ivory spencer and a comely bonnet, she was the picture of vibrancy and beauty. He increased his pace down the last few stairs.

And then stopped short.

She didn't look nearly as happy to see him as he was to see her. Yet she'd come here.

"My lord, Miss Henwick is here," Goring, his aging butler, intoned.

Henwick? Daniel wouldn't correct the man. "Yes, thank you," he responded with a touch of irony.

Goring inclined his head. "Shall I see her out?"

Not for the first time, Daniel worried the man might be ripe for retirement. He'd discuss it with his secretary.

Daniel gave his butler an encouraging smile. "I think I'll just take her along with me."

"Of course, my lord." Goring took himself off, likely to nap in a chair tucked under the stairs. Yes, probably time to broach the subject of retirement. For the thousandth time, Daniel reflected on the responsibility he now carried and how it had all come to pass.

Then he focused on Jocelyn and was grateful it had. "I'm pleased to see you this afternoon. In fact, I was just on my way to see you."

She blinked, looking a bit startled. "Indeed?" Then her features relaxed into ... relief?

He led her from the foyer up the stairs to the sitting room, which overlooked Brook Street. "Shall I ring for tea?" he asked, thinking he should've just asked Goring for it. One of these days he'd master the nuances of household management.

"No, thank you," she said softly. Then she removed her bonnet and set it on a table near the door.

Daniel moved to help her take off her spencer.

She smiled up at him as he took the garment and laid it over the back of a chair. "Thank you."

The afternoon was bright, and the draperies were open to invite the spring light inside. Sunbeams streaked across her hair, painting the rich brown strands with gold. She tipped her head up at him and the light caught her hazel eyes, illuminating a thin green ring just around the pupil.

She opened her reticule and withdrew an object. Opening her palm, she revealed her father's watch fob.

His insides immediately tensed. "How did you get that?"

"From Lord Aldridge."

Bloody hell, she wasn't just impulsive, she was downright foolish. He didn't bother keeping the sarcasm from his tone. "Somehow I doubt he just brought it to your town house."

She gave a half-smile and her cheeks pinked a bit. "Well, he did. Somewhat. He came to see me, but while I'm happy to have my father's fob back, I don't think it was worth what I had to endure."

Now she was scaring the hell out of him. He moved to stand before her in three quick steps. "What happened?" God help the earl if he'd touched her.

"He told me lies. I hope," she added, her eyes guarded as she looked up at him. There was a darkness to her gaze that raised his hackles.

He urged himself to remain calm. As a constable, he'd learned to maintain his equanimity, and it would serve him well now. "Why don't you start at the beginning?"

He gently touched her elbow and had to fight the urge to pull her against his chest and kiss her senseless. He'd wanted to do that the moment he'd seen her in the foyer, but now, knowing she'd somehow been at another man's mercy, the primitive male inside of him wanted to stamp her as his.

She seemed blessedly unaware of the turmoil in his brain as she allowed him to guide her to the settee. She perched on the edge and he sat beside her—close, but not too close, which was a damned shame.

The fob rested in her palm and she glanced down at it before she spoke. "Aldridge came to see me, and I'm afraid I shared more than I ought."

Her admission did nothing to ease his racing pulse. "What did you do?"

The intensity of her gaze was both alarming and exciting. "I warned him you were compiling evidence against him."

He felt like he'd been kicked in the gut. He was so close to catching Aldridge. All he needed was the note Jagger would intercept and deliver. "You didn't."

The pink in her cheeks flushed darker. "I'm afraid I did,

and he told me I should be worried that you were mounting evidence against *me*."

"He *what?*" He couldn't keep the word from exploding from his mouth. So much for keeping calm.

"He said you were corrupt, that you'd put him into contact with a fence you knew. And then he told me not to say a word about it to you. Indeed, he told me I should stay away from you entirely and return to Kent."

Daniel had learned violence at a relatively young age, thanks to his father's and then his chosen profession. He didn't like to hurt people and tried to avoid it when possible. However at this moment he wanted nothing more than to throttle Aldridge to within a breath of his life.

"I'm not corrupt," he said quietly, just barely keeping his temper in check.

"Of course you aren't." She sounded relieved, as if she'd harbored at least a bit of doubt. Which made the next revelation so difficult.

He steeled himself and said, "I wasn't corrupt, but I wasn't completely honest, either."

Her head snapped up, and her eyes were wide. "What do you mean?"

How to explain this so a layman would understand? "Constables sometimes have to do things, no, that's not quite right. *I* sometimes had to do things ... No, that isn't right either."

He turned from her and frowned at the smoldering coals in the fireplace. If he was going to confess his sins, he may as well do it right. He positioned his body toward her, setting one arm on the back of the settee. "I sometimes chose to ignore certain crimes and use lesser criminals in order to snare a larger one."

She cocked her head to the side, considering his words. "I suppose that makes sense. I'm sure you did what you thought was right."

His fingers curled around the top of the settee, uncomfortable with her ready acceptance. "I'm not sure it was. I did what I thought I had to, but some of the things I ignored ..." When he thought of the people he'd allowed to go free—

people like Nicky Blue who recruited children, some of them only seven or eight years old—he despised himself. He took small comfort in having sent Nicky Blue to prison for a time, but it wasn't enough. It was why reform was so important to him now. More police meant more enforcement. They wouldn't have to rely on the criminal class to do so much of their jobs for them. And prison reform would help inmates choose a better path when they were released, so they wouldn't simply return to their illegal and violent ways.

She turned and set her hand on his, and her gentle touch coaxed his fingers to loosen their grip on the settee. "It doesn't sound like corruption to me. You weren't furthering your own interests, were you?"

God, she understood. He searched her face, seeking the absolution he could really only give himself. Still, her perception set a fire of longing deep in his heart.

He shook his head. "No. I thought I was doing what was right."

"Then it was. You were willing to overlook my thievery—something for which I am deeply grateful." She took a moment to strip her gloves off and drop them on the low table set before the settee. Then she settled further back into the settee, and her warm hand was back caressing his. Her fresh apple scent curled its way around him. "You're a good man, Daniel Carlyle."

"Then you don't believe anything Aldridge told you?" She'd trusted him implicitly, had come here straightaway despite Aldridge's lies. Daniel felt like a cad for doubting her when Aldridge had tried to fill his head with nonsense about her.

She made an unladylike sound that sounded rather liked a snort. "Of course not."

He turned his hand over, capturing hers. His energy shifted from tense anxiety and remorse to being enthralled by her presence and sensitivity. "Why not? What have I done to earn your trust?"

She looked at him, her beautiful hazel eyes wide and trusting. "Only protected me, believed in me. For heaven's sake, I used you to get close to Aldridge so I could steal my possessions back! I should be asking you what I've done to earn *your* trust."

Just as she'd said, he trusted her because she believed in him. She saw good in him and understood what he'd never dared to share with anyone else. Which made his next admission necessary, albeit unpleasant. "I'm ashamed to say Aldridge also tried to poison me against you. He said you'd been disdained during your Season, that your reputation was marked by your rash tongue—which I have no trouble believing and have begun to rather appreciate—and a somewhat, ah, loose nature."

She gasped. "Never say so."

He deserved her outrage. "I didn't want to believe it. But I've known him much longer than I've known you, and we were friends." His ire spiked when he thought of his "friendship" with a criminal. "I should've known right away he was lying."

"He told you this last night, before I saw you. That was why you left like you did." Her voice sounded hollow as she withdrew her hand. "After the way I kissed you ... You believed I was soiled."

Cad wasn't a strong enough word to describe him. He'd been an utter ass. "I was a fool." He rubbed his thumb along her jawline. "You are a spirited, intelligent woman who isn't afraid to pursue what she wants. You are a singular female. One I am honored to know. I humbly beg your forgiveness."

She blinked rapidly, but he caught a glimmer of moisture in her eyes. "There's no need to beg," she murmured.

"I think I must. In fact ... " He slid from the settee onto his knees. He took both of her hands in his and stroked his thumbs along the backs. She shivered from his touch, and he longed to see her entire body react when he at last made love to her.

"Miss Renwick, I most humbly beg you to be my wife. I'm perhaps not entirely worthy of your esteem, but I shall endeavor to be so, if you'll but consent. Can you accept a flawed man with a past so different from your own?"

She let his question hover a moment—did she know how she tortured him? "I think I can." She sounded so serious that his breath caught with a mixture of dread and anticipation. "On one condition."

He'd deliver the moon if it meant she'd be his. "Anything."

"Would you mind closing the door?"

Chapter Ten

IT WAS a brazen request, but he'd said he liked her independence. Or something like that. He'd proposed marriage, and that meant he liked her just the way she was. She needn't rein in her tongue or tiptoe around her desires. She was free to be the woman she wanted to be.

He blinked at her once. Then his lips curled into a smile, and he got up and closed the door firmly. He stalked to the windows and pulled the drapes—*how thoughtful.*

When he turned back to the settee, his features had sobered. His gaze had turned intent, the blue-gray irises piercing with their usual fervor. She'd thought she could lose herself in them, and now she wanted to see if she could lose herself in *him.*

Her pulse was already speeding, but it ticked up another notch as she considered what she was about to do. She wasn't afraid or concerned, but happy to share this with him—a kind and honest man who exceeded every dream she'd had.

She scooted to the edge of the settee. "What should I do?"

He sat beside her. "Whatever you like." He trailed a finger along her temple and behind her ear, causing her to shiver in anticipation. "I want to take your hair down, but I don't think that's wise. You probably shouldn't go home looking ravished."

His words heated her, sending warmth spiraling through her veins. An ache started in her belly and moved lower. "And is that how I'll look?"

"You could, but I don't think Mrs. Harwood would approve. We should perhaps be a bit more discreet. I shall endeavor not to muss your hair. That is, if you truly want to do this." He searched her face. "We can wait until after we're married."

She cupped his face in her hands. "No, I don't want to wait. I want you right now. Right here. Tell me what to do. Show me."

He slid his hand around to her nape and pulled her close. His nose nudged her cheek just before his lips found hers. The kiss was soft, gentle, not at all what she craved. The fire he'd started inside of her begged to be stoked. She angled her head and slid her hands further back along his cheeks and jawline. His flesh was hot and smooth, and he smelled of clove. She opened her mouth, eager to taste as well as feel him.

He answered her need with his tongue, sweeping into her mouth with precision and heat. Then he suckled her tongue, and the sensation was shockingly wonderful. She gravitated toward him, pressing her breasts against his chest. But there were too many clothes between them. She wanted to feel his bare skin.

She slid her hands down his neck and then began to tug the lapels of his coat open. He knew her intent immediately and shrugged out of the garment. All the while, his kiss was deep and relentless. Desire curled through her and settled in her core.

His fingers brushed her back and then he broke the kiss. But he didn't move away. He spoke against her lips, nibbling at her mouth between words. "How does," *nibble*, "your dress," *nibble*, "come off?" And then he kissed her again without waiting for her answer, as if he just couldn't help himself. A thrill shot through her, and she smiled into the kiss.

She followed his lead and withdrew momentarily. "It fastens," *kiss*, "in the front." She slanted her mouth over his and renewed the kiss with all the passion coiling inside of her. Then she set to work unfastening her bodice. Thankfully, his hands joined hers because she was having great difficulty concentrating on something so mindless as opening a dress.

Daniel was having no such trouble. In a trice, her bodice was gaping and he pulled it from her shoulders, fully exposing her corset. Then his hands returned to her back, and he tugged the laces until the garment loosened. He skimmed his hands up her arms and slid the narrow straps from her shoulders. The feel of the linen brushing over her sensitive flesh elicited a delicious shiver.

His mouth left hers, and he licked a path to the hollow at the base of her throat. Once there, he lavished her with kisses and nipped at her skin. Her head fell back under his ministration, which thrust her breasts forward in a most wanton way. But she didn't care. She needed more.

His hands slid inside of her corset and cupped the undersides of her breasts. They felt full and heavy, and his touch only increased the sensation. His mouth continued down while he pulled at her chemise, popping her breasts free of the garment. And then his mouth was *there*. Covering her breast with the same delicious wet heat of his kisses. His fingertips tugged at one nipple while he licked and sucked the other. Sensation shot straight to her core and she pressed her legs together to ease the ache between her thighs.

Desperately, she grasped at his cravat, pulling the knot free. As the fabric loosened, his clove scent rushed over her. She inhaled deeply, loving the smell and knowing she would forever associate it with the way he was making her feel—beautiful, desired, powerful.

Suddenly, he pulled back from her and sat up on the settee. "No, no. This isn't right. I can't do this."

Cold air washed over her bare breasts and doused her arousal like a bucket of water from the English Channel. "I beg your pardon?" She blinked at him, not understanding.

He stood.

Disbelief warred with her rising ire. "You are *not* leaving me."

His lips curled into a sinful smile. "No. But you deserve better for your first time." He leaned over and easily swept her into his arms. "My bedchamber is just through here."

He shouldered through a door into a small office and then through another door. This room was quite large and was set at the back of the house. A massive fireplace took up half of one wall and a wide four-poster bed took up half of the opposite.

The ease with which he transported her and carefully set her on the bed made her feel incredibly feminine, or maybe it just heightened his masculinity. Either way, it only added to her arousal. She stood, and now it was his turn to look perplexed.

He frowned. "Where are you going?"

"Nowhere." She kicked her shoes off, shimmied out of her dress, and handed it to him, then followed it with her corset.

The corner of his mouth quirked up and he set the garments on a chair. He was working very hard to keep her from looking ravished, but caution was clearly not her forte. She drew her chemise over her head and tossed it on the floor, leaving her clad in only stockings and garters.

He moved to pick up the chemise, but she clasped his wrist. "Leave it. Show me how this is supposed to be. Make me look ravished. Make me *feel* ravished." She waited for his response, breathless and anxious that she'd gone too far with her brazen tongue.

His gaze raked over her nearly nude body. He reached out and trailed his fingers down her ribcage and over her hip. He kneeled then and slid one finger beneath her left garter. With the flick of his thumb, he undid the fastening and it fell from her leg. Then he languidly rolled the stocking over her knee and down her calf, holding her foot up to remove the silk, and then throwing it heedlessly behind him.

She stifled a grin at his carelessness, enormously glad she hadn't alienated him with her brashness. Then he moved to her other leg, but this time he gripped her thigh with one hand while he removed her garter and stocking. She forgot about everything but the feel of his palm against her flesh and the gentle glide of the stocking from her leg.

When she was truly naked at last, he looked up at her and she had a moment of panic. What was she doing?

He must've seen it, for he paused. Then he pressed a gentle kiss to her hip. "You have only to tell me to stop, and I will. In the meantime, I plan to grant your request. But be warned, ravishment is a serious task meant to be enjoyed. You must tell me what you like and what you don't. What you want and what you don't."

All while he talked, his hand splayed over her sex. His thumb lightly caressed her folds. Her knees quivered as sensations she'd never imagined washed over her.

She managed to find the words to voice what she wanted—since that's what he'd instructed her to do. "I want you naked too."

"Can you wait a moment?" he asked, his focus entirely upon her sex. "I'm just too intrigued by this right now. And I'm afraid," he slid his thumb deeper into her flesh, "I simply can't tear myself away." He leaned forward and she felt the heat of his breath against her. God, he was looking at her in such a way, his fingers touching her as no one ever had ... She could only stare in wonder.

"Spread your legs a bit," he said, so close to her flesh that she felt the words as much as she heard them. She did as he bade. With greater access, he slid his thumb up and found a spot so delicate, so sensitive, that the slightest touch jerked her hips forward. She squeezed her eyes shut for a brief moment as pleasure rocketed through her body.

"You are every bit as responsive as I imagined. A woman like you is bound to be passionate. Show me, Jocelyn. Show me how much."

He worked his thumb over her, teasing that nub until her flesh began to quiver and the desire in her core heated to an unbearable degree. He clasped her hip and lifted her to sit on the edge of the bed. Then he pressed her thighs wide, completely opening her to him now. She could only stare in hopeless abandon as his thumbs met at her core. He stroked her softly but purposely and then opened her. His head ducked forward and then his tongue was on her, licking her flesh in the most intimate kiss.

He guided her legs over his shoulders, cupping the backs of her thighs. His kiss deepened, becoming a series of sucks and licks that worked her flesh in increasing waves of pleasure. She was losing her sanity with each torturous stroke. A pressure was building inside of her and she sought a release she wasn't sure she could find. She gripped the back of his head, seeking something to ground herself. His tongue swirled over that spot and she arched up.

More. Please.

She groaned and realized, embarrassingly, she'd spoken her pleas aloud. But then she was glad she had because he answered by sliding his finger inside of her. There was a sharp pinch, but it quickly ebbed. She pushed into his thrust and his tongue increased its movement, driving her to the edge of something. He ruthlessly pumped in and out of her, creating a delicious friction. Then he sucked her flesh, and her world shattered.

She cried out, her hips jerking. He held her tightly, his mouth and hand easing her crisis as wave after wave of pleasure rocked her frame. Slowly, the world reformed, but it was brighter, clearer, more beautiful than ever before.

She opened her eyes, having squeezed them shut as she'd fallen from on high. He was looking up at her with those intense eyes, and yes, she'd finally lost herself to him. And she didn't think she ever wanted to be found.

DANIEL stared up at her blissful expression and felt a surge of masculine pride. He'd pleasured plenty of women, but he'd never experienced this bone-deep satisfaction. And this was just giving her pleasure. He nearly shook with want when he imagined how it would be to make love to her.

Her cheeks were flushed, her lips parted in wonder. She did look a bit ravished, but he could do far better. The question was, should he? It might be best if they stopped now.

He decided to test the water. "How do you feel?"

"Astonished. I never imagined …" She shook her head dazedly. "I thought we were going to, that is … that wasn't what I expected."

He leaned back on his heels and caressed her still-quivering thighs. "And what were you expecting?"

"You inside of me. On top of me. Our bodies joined."

Her words set fire to his lust. He wanted all of those things and conceived the many ways they could do each one. He was suddenly impatient, wanting to share everything with her now. But there would be a lifetime for them.

He stood. "We can still do that. If you want."

Her lids drooped seductively, and she focused her glorious

hazel eyes on him. "Oh, I want. I think you're overdressed." She slid from the bed to her feet with a speed he didn't think was possible, given the languor that had filled her moments ago.

She pulled the cravat from his neck and then started at the buttons of his waistcoat. He let her strip the garment from him and tug his shirt from his pants. But when her hands pushed the clothing up and skimmed over his bare flesh, he lost all semblance of patience. He grasped the hem of his shirt and pulled it over his head. It had scarcely left his fingertips before he was bent over and pulling his boots and stockings off. Her fingers were on his fall before he stood upright when his feet were finally bare. The buttons came loose and he shoved first his pants from his legs and then his drawers.

She'd stopped moving and was staring at his erection. Damn, he should've waited to remove the drawers. But then her fingers tentatively touched the tip of his penis and he nearly came apart in her hand. No, losing the drawers had been the best idea of his entire life.

"Is this acceptable?" Her question was soft, guarded.

"It's a hell of a lot more than acceptable." He sounded like he'd run up two flights of stairs, but he simply couldn't get a full breath right now. Not when her delicate fingers were sliding over his hot flesh with an innocent precision that was going to drive him mad.

"You're so hard and hot." Her other hand caressed his chest, gliding over his ribcage and abdomen with dizzying effect. Up it went again, toward his nipple. "How does this feel when I touch it? Is it like I feel when you touch me?" She tweaked the nipple between her fingers.

Desire pulsed into his groin. "It feels good. How does it feel for you?" He somehow found the wherewithal to encircle one of her breasts with his hand. He cupped the flesh, palming it and then pulling on her engorged nipple. His mouth filled with moisture and he bent to take her into his mouth.

"Oh. It feels impossibly delightful." She moaned and wrapped her hand around his cock. Her grip was deliciously tight and hot.

He suckled her breast and she arched up into his mouth.

Instinctively, he arched too, sliding his cock along her palm. Her hold didn't loosen and the friction was so sweet he wanted to shout with the joy of it. "Yes," he urged her. "Just like that."

She understood because she began to move her hand. Up to the tip and back to the base. She set a rhythm that had him thrusting into her hand. His balls tightened with each stroke. He needed to put a stop to this unless he wanted to come all over her. The image was erotic and stoked his lust to an even brighter level, but there would be time for that and so many other things. Right now, he wanted to give her what she wanted. Cover her. Join their bodies. Slide inside of her.

Heedless of her damned hair—and the fact that she had to let him go—he picked her up and gently tossed her onto the bed. She gasped in surprise, her eyes widening slightly.

"This is ravishment, darling." He drank his fill of her petite frame, her small, lush breasts, enticingly narrow waist, and the gentle flare of her hips. She was exquisite—and she was his. Pride and gratitude washed through him. He never imagined he'd find a woman like her. Find love.

"Then ravish me. Please." She held up her hand and it was all the encouragement he needed.

With a growl, he climbed onto the bed and moved on top of her, his big body covering hers. He instantly worried about the difference in their sizes. "Am I hurting you?"

She settled beneath his weight, spreading her legs so he could nestle between her thighs. "No. You feel divine." She brushed her breasts across his chest and he felt the graze of her nipples against his flesh. God, she knew just what to do. His curious, fearless, incomparable Jocelyn.

He reached between them and stroked her clitoris. She immediately cast her head back and gave an erotic little whimper. Her thighs fell apart and moisture coated his fingers as he stroked her entrance.

"No. Fair," she said breathlessly.

Her hand came around his cock again and she pumped his length.

"Jocelyn," he ground out. "Put me inside you, darling. I need to feel you." He spread her folds and drove his tip to her opening. "That's it. Just help me slide in."

He'd felt a slight resistance earlier when he'd pushed his finger inside of her, but now she only felt tight. He went slow. God, it was so hard to keep himself from slamming into her, especially with her hand still wrapped around the base of his cock.

Her intake of breath made him go even slower. Sweat trickled down the back of his neck with his effort.

"Tell me if you want me to stop." Heaven help him if she did.

"You're so big."

He smiled at the incredulity in her tone. "Or you're so small."

She made a sound that sounded like a grimace.

He stopped and let her accommodate him a moment. "Ready?"

She nodded beneath him. He slid in further, and she had to move her hand. She skimmed his hip and settled her palm on his buttock, squeezing his flesh as he seated himself fully inside of her. Christ, she was spectacular.

She was so tight and hot. He worried he was hurting her. "Are you sure you're all right?" he asked.

She cupped his cheek with her free hand. "Daniel, I realize I'm a small person and that I'm new at this, but you're not going to break me." She smiled up at him. "I'm quite ready to be ravished."

"Your wish is my greatest desire." He pulled back out of her and pushed forward, keeping his gaze locked with hers. Her eyes widened and her mouth formed an O.

He retreated and drove into her again. Slowly, methodically, forcing her body to accept his. And by the way her legs curled around his hips, she was having no difficulty. After several more strokes, her head fell back and her eyes fluttered closed. She gripped his arse and his shoulder.

Each thrust made her hotter, wetter, until he was sliding in and out of her with ease. She arched her hips to meet him, wordlessly urging him faster. He obliged, thrusting his hips with greater frequency, and angling his cock to exactly stroke against her clitoris. She groaned somewhere deep in her chest and her other hand trailed down his back to clasp him more tightly against her. He could feel her orgasm building by the frantic twitch of her hips and the desperate clutch of her hands.

He pumped faster, answering her need with his own. His balls drew up with his impending release. He reached between them and pressed on her nub. She instantly fell apart, opening her mouth in a series of whimpers and moans that drove him past the brink.

With a final thrust, he spilled his seed into her, his orgasm overtaking him with a white-hot bliss he'd never experienced. He cried out her name and pumped her flesh until he was utterly spent.

Minutes later, he rolled to his side and gathered her close. She turned her head to look at him. Her eyes were slightly glazed, her skin a lush pink, and strands of her hair had come free. She appeared thoroughly ravished. He smiled. They'd get her repaired before he took her home.

"Why are you smiling?" she asked, curling into him.

"Shouldn't I be?"

She smiled in return. "Of course you should. That was wonderful." She peered up at him, suddenly serious. "How long do we have to wait to hold the wedding?"

He laughed. "I'll post the banns this Sunday. You'll need to decide where you want to get married."

"Me? What about what you want?"

He pressed a kiss to her brow. "I want whatever makes you happy. We can talk about it on the way to your house. I really should get you home. Whatever are you going to tell Mrs. Harwood about where you've been?"

"I'll just say we went for a drive in the park. She was napping when I left anyway."

"After you met with Aldridge." He immediately wished he hadn't mentioned him. A dark pall fell over their post-lovemaking bliss.

"Yes." She trailed her finger along his chest, which did a measurable job of distracting him from the damned earl. But then she said, "What are you going to do about him?"

He wasn't sure. Aldridge was now aware that Daniel was investigating him. He could only hope Jagger might still be able to deliver evidence against him, but he accepted the chances were slim. He might be better off going to see him and simply laying things out. And then what?

"Are you going to let him continue his activities?" she asked, verbalizing his inner dialogue.

"If I do, I'm no better than I was. But I don't have evidence against him yet and it may be difficult to obtain."

"Not if he continues. Can't you set some sort of trap?"

He stared down at her in wonder. "You've a deviously sharp mind, do you know that?" She smiled and he kissed the tip of her nose. "I suppose I could do that, but he may be expecting something like that, now that he knows I'm investigating him."

She cringed. "Sorry. I never should have told him."

"It's all right," he said, kissing her and letting his lips linger against hers. His cock was stirring again, which meant they needed to leave right now or her absence would *really* be noted. He kissed her once more, deeply, thoroughly, to last him until he saw her next. Although they did have a ten- or fifteen-minute carriage ride to her town house ...

She sucked on his tongue and wound her fingers into his nape. With a groan, he pulled himself away from her. "We should go."

With a sigh, she stretched, which drew his attention directly to her breasts. "I suppose."

He turned and practically jumped from the bed before he made love to her again.

She sat up and gave him an alluring smile. "How do I look?"

He took in her tousled hair—still pinned up, but with strands jutting every which way—her drowsy eyes, and her kiss-reddened lips. "Ravished."

"Then I thank you, sir."

Incomparable.

Chapter Eleven

SO THIS was what love felt like.

Daniel marveled the entire coach ride home, including the stop he'd made to buy Jocelyn flowers, none of which he could name, and have them delivered to her house. He marveled as he asked Goring to instruct his valet to draw a bath. He marveled as he climbed the stairs and contemplated what sort of engagement ring to purchase and then chastised himself for not getting it first. But then they were apparently going to do everything out of order, given what they'd just done.

Not that he regretted it. Quite the opposite. He'd make love to her again right now if it wouldn't be beastly of him. Maybe tomorrow ... And then he'd tell her he loved her, which he was ashamed he hadn't done today. But then, neither had she.

He stepped into his bedchamber and froze. Jagger lounged in the chair situated in front of the fireplace. "Afternoon," he drawled. "Or is it evening?" He scrutinized Daniel's hastily—and inexpertly—tied cravat. "Just get dressed?"

The lingering bliss of his interlude with Jocelyn faded and was replaced with an edgy excitement. Had Jagger brought the details of Aldridge's latest coded note? "I assume you're here to make a delivery, though I rather wish you hadn't snuck into my bedchamber."

"I'm afraid I'm not here for that." Jagger braced his hands on the arms of the chair. "Nor will I be supplying you with the evidence you sought."

The miserable son of a bitch! Daniel strode toward the intruder and hauled him out of his chair by the front of his coat. "Then what the hell are you doing in my house?"

Jagger found his footing beneath him and stepped back from Daniel, out of his grip. "I beg your pardon, this is a very expensive coat."

"That I'm sure you stole and could replace a hundred times over." How the hell had this bastard gotten into his bedchamber? Daniel had a horrid suspicion this visit had something to do with Jocelyn.

"The latter is quite true, but I must tell you I had this made on Bond Street." Was the prick still jabbering on about his bloody coat?

Daniel advanced on him and raised his hand to grab his lapel again. "I don't give a shit where you shop. Talk before I rip the garment—and you—to shreds."

"Christ, man, there's no need to be offensive. I came here to tell you to stop your investigation of Aldridge."

"No."

Jagger straightened his coat and squared his shoulders. He was of equal height to Daniel, if not a hair or two taller. His gray eyes turned to stone. "I'm not asking."

"And I'm not one of your lackeys." Not anymore.

Jagger showed no indication he'd heard what Daniel had said. "If you want Miss Renwick to be safe, you'll leave Aldridge alone and let the problem resolve itself."

The bastard knew her name? Daniel grabbed him by the lapel again, but Jagger threw him off and withdrew a knife from his boot.

Daniel slid his own knife from its sheath, also tucked into his boot. "Is this really how you want to do this?"

"Not at all, but you don't seem interested in listening to reason. I'm trying to help you here."

"By threatening my fiancée?"

Jagger inclined his head as if they were sharing tea instead of brandishing knives. "Congratulations. Then you really should heed my counsel." He lowered his weapon and raised his other hand in supplication. Then he stowed the knife back in his boot. He blinked at Daniel, clearly waiting for him to do the same.

Daniel complied, but gave him a frigid stare. "Why should I

listen to you?"

"To keep yourself and your fiancée safe. The problem with Aldridge will resolve itself shortly. You can trust me."

Like he'd trust an opium addict. "How is it going to resolve itself?"

Jagger's mouth ticked up at the corner, but there was no humor in the expression. "I don't think you really want to know."

They were going to kill Aldridge? No matter the man's crimes, he couldn't allow Jagger or any of his cohorts to execute him. "I can't let you do that."

"Why, because he's an earl?" Jagger shook his head. "He's been involved with criminal activity for years. Men have hanged for far less than he's done."

Daniel clenched his fists. He wanted to see Aldridge pay for his crimes, but not this way. "That doesn't make it right. He needs to be tried, and then he'll go to prison."

Though he likely wouldn't serve a great sentence, it didn't matter. His criminal career was quite finished. Poor Lady Aldridge—was she aware of her husband's crimes, or was she as innocent in all of this as Jocelyn?

Jagger narrowed his eyes. "You're missing the point. Gin Jimmy isn't going to risk Aldridge being tried." Because he'd bring more of Gin Jimmy's operations to light.

Daniel tried to appeal to Jagger's own sense of survival. "Why do you care so much about Jimmy? One of these days, he's going to fall, and surely that would benefit you."

Jagger's sharp laugh filled the room. "Not bloody likely. I don't want his job." He sobered and stared Daniel square in the eye. "There's nothing you can do to stop what's been ordered. And if you try ... Well, you're familiar with Gin Jimmy's tactics."

Cross him, and you were marked for life. Fear for Jocelyn burned Daniel from the inside out. "If he harms Miss Renwick, I will hunt him down and gut him."

Jagger arched an ebony eyebrow. "I believe you've made your feelings regarding Miss Renwick quite clear. So do what you must to keep her safe."

"I don't trust Gin Jimmy. Or you."

"At this point, we're your allies. She's in far greater danger from Aldridge than us. Let us do what we do, and you can sail off into your happily ever after."

The bastard was right. Aldridge was a massive threat. Though Daniel had stationed a Bow Street constable on Hertford Street, it wasn't enough. He needed to get to her posthaste.

AFTER taking a quick, restorative bath and dressing for the Pellinghams' dinner party, Jocelyn floated down the stairs. Gertrude was awaiting her in the sitting room off the foyer. Her head encased in an orange turban and her still-slender form draped in a matching gown, Gertrude looked every bit the Society matriarch she was. Widowed these past twenty years and childless to boot, she took great pleasure in visiting London for the Season, and Jocelyn was only too glad she'd had the privilege to serve as her companion this year.

"Good evening, dear," Gertrude said with an assessing perusal. "You look lovely this evening. That color is very becoming on you, even if it's not wholly appropriate."

Jocelyn knew a scarlet gown was risky, but she'd loved this fabric so much when she'd seen it on Bond Street two years ago that she'd used almost all of her pin money at the time to purchase it on the spot. She'd finally had it made into a gown last month when she'd learned she would be accompanying Gertrude to town, but she hadn't had the courage—or necessity—to wear it until now.

Now that she was no longer attached to the wall. She could scarcely wait for Daniel to see her.

Gertrude tapped her lip. "But it's not the gown. I daresay there's something else behind the sparkle in your eyes and the bounce in your step. Moss said Lord Carlyle took you for a drive in the park today."

She could at least share with Gertrude one part of the day's events. In fact, she was fairly bursting with it. "Lord Carlyle has asked me to marry him."

Gertrude's sherry-colored eyes widened as her mouth broke

into an ecstatic grin. "Goodness, so soon? You've only just met."

"I know, it happened rather quickly, I think. But I love him and he loves me." He hadn't said so, but neither had she. And since she knew she was in love with him, it had to be that he felt the same.

Didn't it?

A niggling sense of doubt wandered the recesses of her mind, looking for a place to root and grow, but she shoved it away. She believed in Daniel and their future together.

Gertrude smiled broadly. "Then I am beyond delighted for you, my dear! Whatever will my great-nephew say?"

He'll be happy to have his ward taken care of, Jocelyn thought. It wasn't that he found her a burden, but she knew her guardian would be relieved she was settled. As would any parental figure.

Papa.

Her heart clenched as she thought of how happy her father would be to see her not only marrying a viscount, but marrying for love, as he had done. She hoped he was looking down on her and seeing every happy moment. Well, perhaps not *every* moment.

"Daniel is going to write to Arthur immediately so that the banns may be posted this Sunday."

Gertrude's head bobbed. "Wonderful. Where will you marry?"

They'd discussed the wedding on the ride from Carlyle House. "We decided on Carlyle Hall, since it's to be our home."

There was a knock at the door, followed by Moss's footsteps across the entry hall. Jocelyn wondered if Daniel had returned for some reason. He'd already had flowers delivered. Perhaps he'd sent something else. Expectantly she turned, and the smile blooming on her face died.

A tall, slim man with mangy blond hair filled the doorway of the sitting room. He grinned, revealing a missing tooth in the upper right side of his mouth. "Evenin', ladies."

Sounds of a scuffle filled the foyer and spilled into the sitting room. Hearing Moss's muffled protests, Jocelyn's heart leapt into her throat. She moved forward. The tall intruder held up his hand. "Stay right here."

Jocelyn's heard pounded. The man's eyes were a bright, piercing blue. Could he be Nicky Blue? Her gaze dropped to his hand and there, in his grip, was the knife she'd found in her bedchamber.

He followed her line of sight and held up the blade. "I must thank you for returnin' this, love. I was pretty upset when it went missin'."

Had Daniel given it back to him? When? How? Most importantly, why?

A trio of men dashed past the sitting room doorway. They were trailed by another trio carrying a thrashing Moss. Good for him for not going down without a fight. She meant to do the same. But oh, how her heart ached for Moss and the others going through this again. Though anguish tore at her insides, she elevated her chin and stared frigidly at Nicky Blue.

Beside her, Gertrude began to shake. "Oh, my dear lord! What are you going to do?" Her voice came out as a high-pitched squeak.

It was one thing to terrorize the servants, but an old woman? Jocelyn took her hand in a fierce grip. She spoke in a low tone close to the woman's ear. "We're going to be fine. I promise."

Nicky Blue jabbed a thumb toward Gertrude. "*She'll* be fine. You? We'll just have to wait an' see." He laughed then, a horrid sound that had little to do with amusement and everything to do with intimidation. Or perhaps he was amused by their intimidation.

Though fear spiked through her, Jocelyn refused to be cowed. She put her arm around Gertrude, drawing her close. The older woman was quivering. Jocelyn wanted to beat Nicky Blue into the floorboards for causing her such distress. She settled for stating the obvious. "You're a horrible person."

"Oh, I'm not all that bad." He sauntered forward and leered at her. "Mayhap I'll show ye later on."

Gertrude gasped. "You can't talk to her like that!"

Nicky Blue directed a malevolent stare at Gertrude. "I can do whatever I wish. Mayhap I'll change my mind about ye bein' fine."

Jocelyn stepped in front of Gertrude. "Leave her alone."

Two men stomped into the sitting room and came toward them. Jocelyn put her arms back in a protective stance in an effort to block them from Gertrude.

Nicky Blue reached forward and pulled Jocelyn out of the way by her upper arm. "Time to go."

The other men grabbed Gertrude.

Jocelyn struggled against Nicky's grip, sending her elbows and feet flying in every direction trying to hit him. "Don't hurt her!"

Gertrude turned a ghastly shade of white as they hauled her from the room. Tears burned Jocelyn's eyes as she watched, helpless.

Nicky wrapped her in a tight hug, pinning her arms to her sides, and dragged her forward.

She tried to dig her feet into the floor. "Where are you taking me? Why are you even here?"

"Just doin' my job, love." He turned her around, and his stale breath fanned her face. "And I do love my job."

Jocelyn's grip on reality snapped. She spat in his face and slammed her foot down on his. Then she shoved at his chest. Shocked, he released her and fell back. She spun on her heel, intending to get to the scullery to help Gertrude and the others. But his hand snaked around her waist. She kicked back at him and screamed, hoping a neighbor might hear the disturbance.

He grunted as she connected with some part of him, but he didn't let her go this time. His grip tightened on her waist, bruising her. Then he wound his other hand in the hair pinned atop her head and pulled her backward. Her scalp and eyes burned as he forced her head back so she had to look up at him.

"Stop. Now. Or I'll make ye sorry ye didn't." The leer was back, and this time he added the perversion of licking his lower lip and staring at her breasts. His meaning was quite clear. Still, she couldn't give up. She swung her arms to hit him, and he pulled her hair even harder. Tears squeezed from the corners of her eyes and trailed back along her temples.

"Ye're a right bitch, aren't ye? If ye don't stop, I'll make sure yer precious old lady doesn't see the mornin' light."

That did it. Jocelyn went limp. It was one thing to threaten her, but another matter entirely to cause harm to Gertrude. "You're a monster," she breathed.

"Ready?" The query came from the foyer.

"Just about." He turned her so that her chest was against his, and he pushed her head up. For a moment she was petrified he was going to kiss her. Nausea crept up her throat, but she swallowed against the sensation. Tossing up her accounts all over him would only mean trouble for Gertrude.

"Now," he said menacingly, his eyes boring into hers, "come along quietly or we'll march right down to the scullery and make a mess. Nod if ye understand."

She nodded, hope dying in her breast. Who would even know something had happened? When they didn't appear at the Pellinghams' tonight, Daniel would certainly come calling, but by then it may be too late. Wait, the Bow Street Runner outside! How had the men gotten past him? Her stomach knotted. Had they done something unthinkable to him?

They moved through the foyer. Though she went along with them for Gertrude's sake, he kept a tight grip on her elbow. She was certain he could snap it in two if he chose.

Outside, she quickly scanned for the Runner who typically walked up and down Hertford Street. On occasion, he turned up Park Lane and came back. She didn't see him anywhere.

"Lookin' for yer Runner?" Nicky asked right next to her ear. "He's busy with an accident on Park Lane. Too bad for ye." He cackled as he had earlier, the sound eliciting a shudder through Jocelyn's frame.

And then she was thrust into a hackney coach. Thick curtains blocked the windows, but a small lantern hanging inside illuminated the space.

Nicky and one of the other men climbed inside with her, while the others clambered up top. The coach moved forward in the direction of Park Lane.

"Where are we going?" she asked with a serenity she didn't feel. She had to stay calm if she had any hope of making it through the night.

The lantern cast sinister shadows over his long face. "Someplace special that I like."

God, was he abducting her simply to have his way with her? Her stomach turned, and nausea threatened once more. "Why are you taking me? I don't understand." She *hoped* she didn't understand, but was afraid she did.

He shrugged. "Ye'll have to ask yer Lord Carlyle."

Daniel was behind this? A hollow ache in her chest replaced her nausea. She couldn't believe it, not after everything they'd been through. He'd been nothing but forthright and honest, sharing with her his most private thoughts, his deepest regrets, and his fondest desires. He wouldn't do this.

Aldridge's warning came back to her: *I'd also advise you not to mention what I told you to anyone, especially Carlyle. Those who have suggested his behavior is less than lawful have sometimes disappeared.*

Though her heart told her it couldn't be true, her mind said she'd already disappeared.

Chapter Twelve

THE RIDE to Hertford Street seemed to take a fortnight. By the time Daniel finally arrived, he'd almost convinced himself he was being foolish.

Almost.

He took the steps two at a time and rapped sharply on the door. When no answer was forthcoming, his apprehension vaulted into full panic. He threw open the door and surveyed the empty foyer. He peered into the sitting room, but naught was amiss.

Withdrawing his blade from the sheath in his boot, he crept along the corridor to the back of the house and the stairway leading down to the scullery. He hoped to God that Moss would pop out at any moment, but he feared he would find he and the others bound together as he'd done before. He only prayed it wasn't worse.

Light from the kitchen and scullery below illuminated the stairs. He descended cautiously but quickly, as dread gathered in his veins.

As expected, the servants were tied in a circle, their backs to each other, their mouths gagged. He counted four people. Three servants plus who? The orange turban told him it was Mrs. Harwood. He looked at the top of their heads, seeking Jocelyn's golden brown locks.

She wasn't there.

Rage and fear flooded him, but he forced himself to drop down and first remove the rags from the women's mouths. Then he removed Moss's gag and set about untying him so he could help free the women.

"Oh, thank goodness you arrived, my lord," Moss twisted to give Daniel better access.

Daniel didn't have patience for the knots, so he used his knife to simply cut them all loose. "Where is Jocelyn?" he asked of all and sundry.

Mrs. Harwood sniffed. "They took her, my lord!" She erupted with a large sob, followed by another.

Nan went to comfort the older woman.

Furious energy raced through Daniel, making it extremely difficult to stand still. He wanted to move, run, wreak havoc. "Do you know where? Or who they were?"

Mrs. Harwood shook her head. "The leader was very tall with light, dirty hair." She wrinkled her nose and swiped a handkerchief across it. "And the bluest eyes, but they were terrifying, my lord." She shuddered.

Nicky Blue.

It had to be. The description was too accurate and he'd been here before. "Moss, was this the same man who invaded the house the other day?"

"Yes, my lord." He looked abashed. "I'm sorry."

"It's not your fault, Moss."

"I can't stay here any longer," Mrs. Moss cried, burying her face in her husband's lapel.

"Of course not," Daniel said, somehow finding the composure to address the woman's well-founded fear. "Moss, use my coach and take everyone to my house in Brook Street. Pack some things as none of you will be returning tonight—or at all, if you so choose. I'll find another situation for all of you. Indeed, I may be in need of a butler very soon myself."

Moss nodded as he patted his wife's back. "Thank you, my lord. Your kindness is a blessing."

"Have you any idea at all where they might have taken her?" Daniel asked, his need to find Jocelyn and punish Nicky Blue overtaking every other consideration.

The butler shook his head sadly. "No, my lord. I'm very sorry."

Daniel's thoughts had already shifted to how he would find

them. He had to find Jagger. He turned to go, but then stopped as a thought struck him. He spun back around. "What the devil happened with Bow Street? Isn't someone on patrol?"

"I don't know, my lord," Moss said. "I saw him earlier, but he must not have witnessed the criminals' arrival."

Goddamned amateurs. He should've employed someone from Queen Street for the task. "I'll tell my coachman to expect you," he said. "I'm going to find Jocelyn."

Mrs. Harwood blew her nose. "Please do, my lord. I can't abide anything happening to that lovely girl."

He pressed his lips together and gave a single nod. "We are in agreement, Mrs. Harwood."

She looked up at him and raised her chin. "And I intend to dance at your wedding!"

Their wedding. Anguish and fear threatened to overcome the fury driving his thoughts, but he couldn't give in to those emotions. In fact, he needed to set aside his anger so he could focus on fixing this problem. Jocelyn was counting on him, and no assignment had ever been more important. He forced a smile he didn't at all feel. "I shall count on it."

Night was falling as Daniel made his way to St. Giles in a hired hack. He'd located the errant Bow Street officer who'd been busy with a disturbance on Park Lane, which had surely been orchestrated by Nicky Blue as a distraction. Daniel had briefly considered asking the officer to join him, but some boys were still causing trouble further down the street.

The coach took him directly to the Crystal. He suspected Jagger kept a suite of rooms at the flash house as one of his many residences. He could only hope the criminal had returned after leaving Daniel's town house earlier.

Once inside, Daniel immediately sought out the proprietor, a squat, particularly cynical fellow whom he found easily behind the bar.

"Gaunt," he called.

The stocky man turned and scowled. "I saw ye in here the other night. I thought ye were done bein' a constable."

"Where's Jagger?"

Gaunt made a show of looking about the common room.

"Ye see him here?" Then his irritated gaze settled on Daniel. "Me neither."

He started to turn, but Daniel reached across the bar and pulled the man's shoulder. "Which room upstairs? And don't lie. I'll tear every corner of this place apart until I find him."

"Ye would too, ye prick." He jerked away from Daniel. "One floor up, back corner away from the main stairs. He's got men."

Daniel expected nothing less. Without a word he went to the staircase in the corner of the common room and rapidly ascended. At the landing, he strode down a narrow corridor to the end where two men loitered. One was sitting in a chair but sprang to his feet while the other, lounged against the wall, perked up a bit but didn't alter his lazy stance.

Giving both men a harrowing glare, Daniel put his hand on the doorknob.

"Hold there," the formerly seated man said, setting his hand on Daniel's forearm.

Daniel wasn't going to take time to reason with these men. He drew his blade from his boot and slid it against the flesh below the man's ear. "Open the goddamned door."

The man against the wall lunged for Daniel, but he kicked out and caught him in his gut. Air whooshed out of him in a great gust and he staggered back. Daniel pressed the knife more firmly against his captive's neck. "I said *open the door.*"

He complied, turning and throwing the door open. Daniel pushed the man back into his chair and stepped into Jagger's suite. "Don't bother us." Then he slammed the door closed.

Jagger—shirtless and carrying a small cloth as if he'd just been washing—came striding from another room, his eyes spitting fire. "What the bloody hell are you—" He halted upon seeing Daniel. "Doing here," he finished, his features cooling into mild anger.

"Where is my fiancée, you rat bastard?"

Jagger whipped the cloth over his shoulder, letting it rest upon his bare flesh. He shook his head. "I don't know what you're talking about. I told you what you needed to do to protect her."

"A couple of hours ago! I haven't had time to do a goddamned thing since then."

"Which is why you should realize I had nothing to do with this. I'd guess Aldridge got to her, wouldn't you?"

He couldn't argue with the man's logic. "Nicky Blue took her. I thought he worked for you."

Jagger didn't confirm that, but Daniel never expected him to, at least not without duress. "I didn't realize he was that close with Aldridge." He frowned deeply. "That's troubling."

Daniel didn't give a damn about the problems within their criminal business. His only concern right now was Jocelyn. "Where would he take her?"

Jagger ran a hand through his hair. "Any number of places."

Daniel's patience was growing thin. "Narrow them down, please. I don't have much time." Jagger's gaze dropped to the knife still in Daniel's hand. Daniel shook his head. "Don't ask me to put it away. I'll do whatever I must to get the information I need."

"You see how easily our moral compasses can be skewed?"

Of course he did. His had bent long ago. "I'm not trying to save myself. Try to improve your own morality, and help me save her."

Jagger closed his eyes a moment and when they opened, there was a glimmer of regret. But it was gone so fast, Daniel wondered if he imagined it.

"Try Field Lane. His favorite receiver has a flash house there. Nicky keeps a room and sometimes uses the topmost floor for storage after a job." It was the plainest information Daniel had ever obtained from the likes of Jagger. Given the resignation in the man's eyes, Daniel didn't doubt its veracity for a moment.

"Thank you."

He rushed out, barreling along the corridor and down the stairs as if the building were on fire. A few minutes later he'd directed the hack to Field Lane and could only pray he wasn't too late.

JOCELYN had fought her captor with everything she had, but in the end Nicky Blue had proved far stronger. Plus, he'd had help. Despite that, she'd managed to blacken one bloke's eye and had bitten Nicky Blue's hand hard enough that he'd hauled off and slapped her a moment later. Her cheek still stung.

Bound to a chair, she'd watched evening blend into night through the dingy window of the small room they'd locked her in. They'd left her in the dark, and she was now growing chilled in her capped sleeves.

She knew in her heart Daniel would try to find her. Nicky had tried to convince her Daniel was behind her abduction, but she didn't believe him. She trusted Daniel and knew without a doubt he wasn't a villain. Furthermore, Aldridge was a proven liar, so she simply couldn't credit anything he said. It made far more sense he was the man behind this.

But none of that was any consolation. She still didn't know why she was there or what they had planned for her. And so she shivered with cold and fear.

The door opened, and several men entered carrying lanterns. She blinked against the sudden flood of light. Because of the adjustment, she couldn't see any of their faces.

"How forlorn you look at last, Miss Renwick. I'd begun to wonder if anything could wear you down."

Dread iced her spine as she recognized Lord Aldridge's voice.

"I may look a fright, my lord, but don't let that fool you," she said with a bravado she didn't necessarily feel.

"You are an extraordinary female, I'll give you that. It's no wonder Carlyle was smitten with you. Too bad nothing will come of it."

"You're wrong. Daniel is going to come for me, and we plan to be married."

"Well, you're right about one of those things. He is coming for you, but I doubt he'll have you after I'm finished." His words sent a shaft of stark fear straight through her heart.

Her eyes were now accustomed to the light, and she could see four men, still holding their lanterns, standing just inside the door. Aldridge pulled up a chair and sat directly in front of her.

"This is what's going to happen," he said, his tone as condescending as ever. "You're going to tell Carlyle you stole from me and sold the items for money. You'll also tell him everything you said about me was a fabrication to discredit me in his eyes."

Jocelyn stared at him—he was demented. "He won't believe me. I have no reason to steal from you or recant what I told him, and he knows it. He's an awfully good investigator, or didn't you know that? Perhaps if you did, you would've been smarter about all of this."

Aldridge paled, and his mouth tightened with fury. "Your tongue is going to get you into trouble one day, gel. Be careful today isn't that day." He leaned forward and bared his teeth. When he next spoke, he stressed his words so forcefully that spittle flew from his mouth. "You've practically ruined everything, you little bitch, but I've been trying to avoid having you killed. I've particularly tried to avoid having Carlyle killed. Messy business taking down a viscount. But I'll kill him—and you—if you don't make him think I'm innocent. I plan to confess that I purchased your items from a receiver, but I shall be so full of remorse that even Carlyle will let me be."

She gaped at him. "You're mad. You can't continue. Daniel won't allow it. He knows your scheme, how you inform criminals like Nicky Blue as to what town house he should rob and when. And you do it to obtain specific items, sometimes from people you even call friend." He'd explained everything to her on the carriage ride to her town house earlier. Her heart had broken at the betrayal in his voice. "Daniel will never believe you only purchased the stolen items."

"Then, unfortunately you'll both die."

"Lookee what I found!" Nicky Blue pushed into the room trailed by a pair of men who were holding a struggling Daniel.

Jocelyn instinctively tried to jump up from the chair, but her bonds held her fast.

"Let her go, you son of a bitch," Daniel growled.

Aldridge's back had been to the door, but he got up and faced Daniel. If Daniel was surprised by the earl's presence, he didn't show it. His expression was all malevolence. Jocelyn shivered at the depth of rage in his eyes.

Aldridge cleared his throat. "Carlyle, I'm sorry it had to come to this. I've been trying to spare both of your lives—I'm no murderer—but I'm afraid you've made it quite difficult. Now that you know how the operation works, you can't be allowed to expose it."

"Just tell me why," Daniel said, fury burning in his eyes. "You have wealth, position, a wife who loves you. Why resort to thievery?"

Aldridge took one step toward Daniel. "I have a young wife who likes pretty things and didn't have the funds to appease her. There are certain trappings a countess expects, and her husband must provide them for her. I don't expect someone like you to understand." He cocked his head to the side. "I don't suppose I could ask you to simply look the other way? Perhaps if I delivered you another criminal, say Nicky Blue here? That is how you prefer to conduct this sort of business, isn't it?"

Daniel lunged forward, but Nicky Blue beat him to it. The criminal moved to stand in front of the earl. They were of equal height, but the earl was actually bigger, with broader shoulders and a thicker waist. "Ye won't be doin' that, my lord."

"Count the number of men here." Aldridge inclined his head toward the four men holding the lanterns. "Mine outnumber yours."

"*Yers?*" Nicky asked incredulously. "Who do ye think these blokes work for? Not me, not you. They work for Gin Jimmy. And Gin Jimmy's already given them their orders."

Jocelyn couldn't see Aldridge's face, but she felt the energy in the room shift. Her gaze swung to Daniel, who began to fight his captors even more.

"No," Daniel cried. "Don't do this."

"I have my orders," Nicky said, with more than a touch of glee. He pulled a blade from inside his coat. Its familiar dragon hilt glinted in the lantern light. He delivered Aldridge a look of pure menace. "Take off yer coat."

"Don't," Aldridge said weakly. "I can fix this."

Nicky waved his knife from one of his men toward

Aldridge. The men pulled at Aldrige's sleeves. Though he tried to fight them, they removed the garment, then held his arms.

Nicky moved close to him. "Ye tried and failed." He lifted his hand and slowly pierced the earl's side, sliding the knife in deep. The earl gasped and his hands clenched. "There now, it doesn't hurt too much, does it?" He turned the blade and then withdrew it. "Here, sit down. It'll be over soon."

The two men let go of Aldridge's arms, and Nicky guided him back to the chair so that he was once more sitting in front of Jocelyn.

She stared, horrified, as all color drained from his face. Blood spread over his waistcoat and streamed down his side over the edge of the chair and dripped onto the floor. She made a sobbing sound, but couldn't seem to force her eyes closed. "Help him," she said, but the words came from a distance, as if someone else had uttered them.

"You piece of shit," Daniel yelled.

The earl's eyes settled on her. "I'm sorry," he murmured. Then his mouth sagged, and he slumped in the chair. His gaze unfocused and his lids drooped, but didn't close. Then he was still.

Blood continued to pour from his wound. It began to spread on the floor and slithered toward her like a living thing.

She tried to push the chair back, but it only wobbled and she worried it would tip over.

"You sick son of a bitch," Daniel said.

Nicky snapped his fingers, and two of the lantern men put down their lights. They came and dragged Aldridge to the side of the room. Then the two men holding Daniel brought him forward and tried to sit him in the bloody chair, but he fought them with everything he had.

"A little help," Nicky said, and the men who'd taken Aldridge away returned. "Carlyle needs some persuasion."

Suddenly Jocelyn felt a cold blade against her neck, and Daniel instantly stilled. The men settled him in the chair. She could see his beloved face so close.

"Yer turn," Nicky Blue said, wiping the blood from the knife on Aldridge's discarded coat. "I've been lookin' forward to this for a long time. Ever since ye sent me to the hulks."

Jocelyn shook her head, as horror turned her extremities to ice. "No. Please. No."

The men removed Daniel's coat. He kept his gaze locked with hers. "It's all right, darling." His voice was soothing, calm, but it did nothing to stop the sheer terror gripping every part of her. "I love you."

Tears filled her eyes, and she couldn't draw a deep enough breath to fill her lungs. "I love you too."

His eyes never left hers, but his voice took on a vicious edge. "Nicky, if anything happens to her, I'll find a way to come back and eviscerate you."

Nicky laughed, then came forward.

Jocelyn couldn't bear to watch Daniel die. She squeezed her eyes shut and prayed for a miracle.

Chapter Thirteen

DANIEL TENSED. He was glad Jocelyn had closed her eyes. It was bad enough she'd had to sit there and watch the life drain away from Aldridge, but to force her to watch them murder him too ... If there hadn't been a knife against her throat, he'd kill every single one of them with his bare hands.

"For Christ's sake, Nicky, knock it off!"

Jagger's thunderous voice filled the space. Jocelyn's eyes flew open. Daniel wanted to turn to see if Jagger was alone, but he couldn't turn away from Jocelyn.

He felt the prick of Nicky's blade against his side, and then it was gone. Nicky had been pulled away, quickly disarmed, and was now being held by the two men who'd been holding Daniel.

Jagger came forward and threw a dark glance at Daniel. "Untie her."

Daniel needed no further urging. He quickly released her from the chair, and she was in his arms clutching his neck in an instant. He held her close, trying to absorb all of her anguish and fear.

Jagger faced Nicky. "What an unbelievable mess. What the hell were you thinking, bringing her here? You were supposed to take care of Aldridge. End of assignment."

Nicky's eyes darted from side to side, assessing his situation. It seemed no one was going to come forward to help him. "She found my knife. I can't have her linkin' me to any of that. Especially when she's attached to this son of a bitch." He jabbed his thumb toward Daniel.

"Those decisions are above you." Jagger spoke as if to a

child. "You do as you're told and nothing else. But then that's why you ended up in prison in the first place, if memory serves. Always getting ahead of yourself, thinking you're above your station."

Nicky's mouth tightened, and his eyes slitted.

Jagger dusted off Nicky's shoulder. "I'm afraid it's the last time you do that." He glanced at the men holding his arms. "You know what to do."

"No!" Nicky began to fight his captors. How the tables had turned. And Daniel couldn't summon even an ounce of compassion. Not after what he'd forced Jocelyn to witness.

They dragged him from the room, shouting and struggling. Jagger turned toward Daniel and Jocelyn, his mouth grim. Then he pivoted back to the rest of the henchmen and glared at them. "Why are you standing there? Go help them."

They scurried from the room like rats from a fire.

"I'm sorry for all of that," Jagger said quietly. He wasn't looking at them, and his voice held a dark, desperate quality. Daniel wondered what was going on.

Then the criminal turned and squared his shoulders. "What you do next is very important."

Jocelyn finally relaxed in Daniel's arms and rested her head against his chest. She slid her arms from his neck and clasped them about his waist, holding him as if her life depended on it.

Daniel eyed Jagger skeptically. "What *should* I do next?"

"Absolutely nothing."

"I beg your pardon?"

Jagger clasped his hands behind his back as if he were delivering a lecture. "After you leave here, go on about your life. Get married. Live happily ever after. Forget what you knew about Aldridge—he's quite paid for his crimes, don't you agree?"

More than, but that didn't make any of this right. "I can't do that."

Jagger's eyes narrowed. "Don't be a fool. Of course you can. I'm not asking you to ignore a crime. The theft ring you uncovered—Aldridge and Nicky Blue—is over." As if to punctuate this declaration, screams came from a nearby room, followed by sudden silence. Jocelyn shivered in his arms and gripped his waist even more tightly.

Daniel couldn't argue with that. But he was shocked that Jagger wasn't killing them. "Why are you letting us go?"

He arched a brow. "Because I can."

Daniel was afraid he knew how this sort of arrangement worked. Jagger was saving his life, and would expect reciprocation some day. "You'll want something from me in the future."

Jagger shrugged. "Aside from keeping my name out of this entire event? Perhaps."

Jocelyn looked at Jagger, and then up at Daniel. "Can we go?"

"There's a hack waiting for you outside," Jagger said.

Daniel nodded, then turned with Jocelyn to go. He paused halfway to the door and looked back at Jagger. "It's still not too late for you to choose a different path."

Jagger gave a small, dark smile. "I'm afraid it is."

Perhaps. Still, he wouldn't forget what this criminal had done for them. He led Jocelyn from the flash house and into the waiting hack, calling the address to the driver as he climbed in.

Inside, she curled against him. "Please don't ever let me go."

He brushed his lips against the top of her head. "Never."

She drew back to look up at him as the coach swung into motion. "How is Gertrude?"

"Shaken, but I think she'll be fine." He allowed himself to smile as he recalled Mrs. Harwood's spirit earlier. Her courage was inspiring. "She's looking forward to dancing at our wedding."

She splayed her hand over his chest. "Must we really wait for the banns? After tonight, I don't want to be without you."

His heart clenched. He didn't want to be without her either, wasn't sure he could. "Then I shall procure a special license, and we'll wed immediately. You'll need to stay at my town house tonight anyway. Mrs. Harwood and all of the retainers are there. Poor Mrs. Moss is never returning to Hertford Street."

She laid her head back down against his chest. "I can't say I blame her. I don't want to return, either."

They fell silent. He stroked her back, and her breathing finally reached an even rate.

"What will happen to Aldridge?" she asked. "His body, I mean."

Daniel was all too familiar with how those sorts of executions played out. They'd find his discarded body somewhere far from here, if it was found it at all. Gin Jimmy's gang might decide to dump him into the Thames, especially since he was an earl. But Daniel rather thought Jagger would ensure the body was discovered. That way, Daniel and Jocelyn wouldn't have to keep his death a secret. "It will turn up."

"That's bound to shock Society."

"I'm sure."

She shook her head against him. "Lady Aldridge will be devastated."

Her concern for the man's wife was touching. It reminded him how much he loved her. He tipped her chin up and gently kissed her. "I love you," he said against her mouth.

She kissed him back. "I love you too. When I think about how close I came to losing—" Her breath caught on a sob.

"Shhh," he kissed her again, wanting to take away all of her pain, wishing she could forget the last hours. "You didn't. And I didn't lose you."

She shuddered in his arms and pulled back. "I'm very glad you're no longer a constable. I'd have to insist you resign."

He'd never imagined a life outside the magistrate's office, but now he couldn't ever see going back. Inheriting the viscountcy had changed his path, but falling in love with Jocelyn had altered it permanently. Now he only saw a future with her. With their children. With her love surrounding them.

He caressed her cheek. "I'd do anything for you."

She nuzzled his hand. "Just love me."

"I do."

Epilogue

September, 1818, London

AFTER ALLOWING his valet to put the finishing touches on his cravat, Daniel went back into the bedchamber he shared with his beautiful wife intending to kiss her goodbye before he left for an appointment at the Home Office. But when he went inside, he stopped short at the sight of Jocelyn sitting in bed, her hair still sleep-tousled, her lips parted as she read the newspaper. Perhaps he had a little time…

She tipped her head up and smiled upon seeing him. "There you are. Ready for your appointment, I see." Her gaze raked him provocatively. "Pity, that."

He suddenly didn't give a fig if he was late. He moved toward the bed.

She rattled the paper in her hands. "I've just been reading about Lord Lockwood—you know, that viscount who hosts those vice parties?"

And now she was talking about vice? Good Lord, he was *never* going to make that appointment. He perched on the edge of the bed and leaned over to press a kiss to her shoulder, exposed by her nightrail, which was hanging askew. "Mmm-hmm," he said, far more concerned with the heat of her flesh and her tantalizing apple scent than with bloody Lockwood.

"Well," she said, sounding frustratingly unmoved by his advances, "it seems Lady Margaret has declared his bastard brother has come to London."

That was enough to make Daniel sit up straight. He tilted

the paper so he could read the article.

*Lady Margaret has declared Mr. Ethan Locke to be the bastard brother of Lord Lockwood. Unlike his infamous, titled brother, Mr. Locke is both charming and elegant. He is already a favorite among the lad*ies.

Son of a bitch.
Before Daniel could pursue further thought on that surprising revelation, Jocelyn's lips were trailing along his jaw and then her teeth were nibbling at his earlobe. "Mmm, you smell so good," she said, inhaling deeply. "Must you leave already?"

The Home Office had requested the meeting. It seemed likely they wanted to offer Daniel an appointment, something he wasn't sure he wanted. He was quite happy at present with his new wife and their life together. "This is an important appointment, unfortunately."

Even so, he couldn't resist cupping her cheek and kissing her senseless. She tasted of chocolate, which she drank most mornings, and desire. Sadly, he didn't have time to take it further. A few moments later, he pulled back.

She sighed against his mouth. "I was planning to call on Lady Aldridge later."

He stroked his thumb along her jawline. "That's very kind of you."

She tossed the newspaper aside. "Not as kind as you telling the authorities that Aldridge let us go."

The earl's body had been found the day after he'd been killed, but Daniel had already reported Jocelyn's abduction, Aldridge's crimes, and Daniel's attempt to save her. To keep Jagger out of the story, Daniel had also told Bow Street that Aldridge had let them go. He figured it would give Lady Aldridge comfort to believe her husband had performed an act of compassion before he'd died. What it meant, however, was that Aldridge's murder was unsolved.

The decision to protect Jagger had been difficult, but Daniel's gut told him it had been the right thing to do. Without the criminal's assistance, both he and Jocelyn would be as dead as Aldridge. Daniel hoped he wasn't wrong, but after reading that newspaper article he would need to be diligent.

Daniel tipped his wife's chin up and kissed her softly on the mouth. "I should go. Please convey my best to Lady Aldridge."

"Of course." She slid her hands beneath his coat and encircled his waist. "Is there any way I can convince you to stay?" She smiled coyly up at him and then licked the top of his throat above his suddenly too-tight cravat.

He stifled a groan. "Only about a thousand. Promise me you'll save all of them for later."

She slid her hands down his hips and stroked over his fall. His cock, already stirring, jerked against his small clothes. This was going to be a very long appointment.

Her hazel eyes glittered in the morning light streaming from a small gap in the draperies. "You have my solemn vow to ravish you within an inch of your life."

He grinned down at her. "I can think of no better torture. Now, give me your mouth so I may sample what you have in store for me."

She cradled the bulge in his breeches and kissed him with hot, wicked intent. Yes, it was going to be a long appointment indeed.

The end

Thank you so much for reading *To Love a Thief*! I hope you enjoyed it! Read on for an excerpt from the next book in the Secrets and Scandals Series:

Never Love a Scoundrel

Vengeance is seductive…
Labeled a lunatic and a reprobate, Lord Jason Lockwood finds solace in debauchery outside the realm of Polite Society. Years after provoking Jason's downfall, his bastard brother rises from the rookeries to emerge as the premier gentleman of the ton. Jason vows to uncover the supposedly reformed criminal's secret motive and use it against him to exact revenge—even if it means using a beautiful young debutante whose only mistake is her relation to the woman who has ensured his family's infamy.

But revenge is sweet
Lady Lydia Prewitt is everything a debutante should be: beautiful, dowried, and in possession of a sterling reputation. But life beneath the thumb of her malicious aunt is eroding Lydia's faith in her peers and in herself. When the scandalous yet seductive Lord Lockwood solicits her help to gain entry into the best ballrooms, she jumps at the opportunity to be more than her aunt's minion. But the revelation of his true purpose and the anger that lies beneath his scarred exterior draws her into his dark past. Intervention doesn't come without a price—can she risk her own future to save his?

The set was finishing. If Lydia was right, a waltz was next. Did Lockwood know how? "It's a waltz," she said.

"Is it?" He sounded careless. "Excellent." His gray eyes looked into hers with an intensity that made her toes curl. What was he about this evening?

She took his arm, and they left the alcove. With each step toward the dance floor, Lydia was aware of attention turning toward them, of heads turning, of conversation ceasing. By the time they took their places and the music started, the ballroom was almost deadly quiet, save the strains of the waltz. As he swept her into the dance, the other couples remained still. For a few moments they moved about the center of the ballroom, his hand at her back, her hand on his shoulder, their fingers clasped. It seemed they were the only things moving in the entire world. Time had ceased to advance. Everyone around them was frozen in some eerie tableau.

But Lydia was most aware of him. His wide shoulders, his warmth, that jagged scar…

"Why do you stare at it so much?" he asked.

She shook her head and raised her gaze to his. "What?"

His eyes contained the same intensity as they had in the alcove. "My scar. You always stare at it." His voice grew soft. "Does it make you uncomfortable?"

"No," she said the word before she even contemplated her reasoning. Why did she stare at it? She wasn't the least bit offended by how it looked. "It makes me sad. I wish you didn't have it. I wish I could make it go away, and not because it disfigured your face, but because it's a reminder of something I'm sure you'd rather forget."

She heard his breath catch. Her heartbeat doubled. Something shifted between them. She knew what it was like to want to forget,to erase memories from your mind and maybe create a history that could make you smile instead of weep. His eyes bored into hers and she thought he understood.

Read an excerpt from chapter one at www.darcyburke.com.
To receive notification of future book releases,
sign up for Darcy's newsletter.

Other Intrepid Reads Authors

Books by Emma Locke

The Naughty Girls Series
The Courtesans
The Trouble with Being Wicked
The Problem with Seduction (Winter 2013)
The Art of Ruining a Rake (Spring 2013)

The Hoydens
The Danger in Daring a Lady (Fall 2013)
The Importance of Being a Scoundrel (2014)
The Hazards of Loving a Rogue (2014)

To receive updates on future book releases, sign up for Emma's mailing list at http://www.emmalocke.com.

Books by Erica Ridley

Historical Romance
Too Wicked To Kiss
Too Sinful To Deny
Born To Bite

Contemporary Romantic Comedy
Love, Lust & Pixie Dust
Wands, Wishes & Genie Kisses (Summer 2013)
Fate, Fire & Demon Desire (Fall 2013)

To learn more about Erica, her books, or to sign up for her mailing list for contests, freebies, and new releases, visit http://www.ericaridley.com.

About the Author

Darcy Burke wrote her first book at age 11, a happily ever after about a swan addicted to magic and the female swan who loved him, with exceedingly poor illustrations. An RWA Golden Heart® Finalist, Darcy loves all things British (except tomatoes for breakfast, or any other time of day, actually) and happy ever afters.

A native Oregonian, Darcy lives on the edge of wine country with her devoted husband, their two great kids, and three cats. In her "spare" time Darcy is a serial volunteer enrolled in a 12-step program where one learns to say "no," but she keeps having to start over. She's also a fair-weather runner, and her happy places are Disneyland and Labor Day weekend at the Gorge. Visit Darcy online at http://www.darcyburke.com where you can sign up to receive her newsletter, follow her on Twitter at http://twitter.com/darcyburke, or like her Facebook page, http://www.facebook.com/darcyburkefans.

Made in the USA
Lexington, KY
15 February 2014